Jericho Walls

Jericho Walls

KRISTI COLLIER

HENRY HOLT AND COMPANY

NEW YORK

I would like to thank the following: Lee Collier and Naomi Kouns for sharing their stories; the Indianapolis SCBWI writer's group—Kim Childress, Kim Bradley, Rebecca Dotlich, Diane Hess, Pat Mirsky, LeAnne Hardy, Margaret King, Janet Walls, and Jan Lindemann; Phil and Karen Collier for talking about what it was like to move from Indiana to South Carolina; the Oconee County libraries in Walhalla, Salem, and Seneca, and the Greenville Historical Society; Trent, who patiently endured the process; and Christy Ottaviano, who took a risk on a novice. Thank you.

Henry Holt and Company, LLC
Publishers since 1866
115 West 18th Street, New York, New York 10011
www.henryholt.com

Henry Holt is a registered trademark of Henry Holt and Company, LLC
Copyright © 2002 by Kristi Collier
Distributed in Canada by H. B. Fenn and Company Ltd.

Library of Congress Cataloging-in-Publication Data
Collier, Kristi. Jericho walls / by Kristi Collier.
p.   cm.
Summary: In 1957, when her preacher father accepts a post in Jericho, Alabama,
Jo wants to fit in but her growing friendship with a black boy forces her to
confront the racism of the South and to reconsider her own values.
[1. Segregation—Fiction.   2. Race relations—Fiction.   3. African Americans—Fiction.
4. Friendship—Fiction.   5. Alabama—Fiction.]   I. Title.
PZ7.C6793 Je 2002   [Fic]—dc21   2001039931

ISBN 0-8050-6521-0 / First Edition—2002 / Designed by Donna Mark

Printed in the United States of America on acid-free paper. ∞

1   3   5   7   9   10   8   6   4   2

To Mom,
who knows what it means to tear down walls,
and in loving memory of
William and Gertha Dennison

—K. C.

"Many women do noble things,
but you surpass them all."

(Proverbs 31:29)

I got to thinking over our trip down the river; and I see Jim before me, all the time, in the day, and in the night-time, sometimes moonlight, sometimes storms, and we a floating along, talking, and singing, and laughing. But somehow I couldn't seem to strike no places to harden me against him, but only the other kind. . . . I was a trembling, because I'd got to decide, forever, betwixt two things, and I knowed it.

—Mark Twain
(from *The Adventures of Huckleberry Finn*)

Jericho Walls

chapter one

Daddy said we were moving because he was the last of an old Carolina family, and it was time he went home. Mama said it was because Daddy was tired after running the Gambling Interests out of Cutter County. I knew it was on account of me busting the nose of Jeremy Williamson Harris the Third.

The moment my fist hit his face, I guessed I was bound for trouble. Jeremy was the son of the richest man in Harrisburg, Indiana, the man who donated the new pipe organ to the church. I was the preacher's daughter.

Jeremy deserved to get hit, no doubt. He was a mean, worthless bully. But I shouldn't have been the one to do the hitting. Any other kid would have gotten in trouble, sure, but then that would be the end of that.

Not only did I get in trouble, but my actions heaped shame upon the Lord Almighty Himself. And if causing that kind of shame ain't the worst feeling in the world, I don't know what is.

One week after the fight, Daddy came home with the news that we were leaving. We'd only been in Harrisburg for two years, and I finally had some good friends. After I beat up Jeremy, the boys let me play basketball at Jed Hopper's farm. He had a regulation court set up between his dad's barn and the fence. The last thing I wanted to do was leave.

I begged and pleaded and swore off fighting and spitting and calling names forever after. I'd never get in trouble again, no, sir. But Daddy was firm. He'd gotten an offer to pastor a church in his hometown of Jericho, South Carolina, and he heard God's call. I myself had never gotten a call from God, but Daddy got one every couple of years, which meant we had to pack up and go.

I'd keep out of trouble in Jericho, I promised myself that hot July day as our blue Chevy groaned over the Smoky Mountains and curved through the rolling hills. I'd do all the right things and make lots of good friends and no one would care a whit about my being the preacher's daughter. At least that's what I hoped would be true.

We arrived in Jericho on a Tuesday. After we'd unpacked our few belongings, Mama and Daddy went straightaway to work—Mama visiting the sick and shut-in, Daddy going to church meetings to find out what folks wanted from him. I poked about, watching the town shimmer in the heavy Carolina haze and listening to the slow drawl of folks who came to visit and gossip and snoop.

I woke early that first Sunday. The sun was barely a stain in the sky, but the air was hot and clammy. My nightgown stuck to my skin. I padded to the bathroom and splashed my face with cold water. My stomach clenched in a queasy ball. I thought about throwing up, then decided it wouldn't do any good. I'd only missed one day of church in my entire life, when I was five years old, and that was because the doctor thought I had polio and told Daddy he'd send him to jail if he exposed me to anybody else. It turned out I only had a bad case of the flu. Mama was furious at that doctor for giving her the scare of her life. I was grateful because I got to stay home and listen to the radio and drink lemonade. Now that they had a vaccine for polio, I couldn't use that as an excuse.

Besides, I knew I wasn't really sick. I only felt sick. It was the same kind of feeling I got every time I had to march myself into a new church.

I dried my face, then walked into the kitchen. Daddy was sitting at the Formica table, drinking black coffee and eating a piece of unbuttered bread and a grapefruit. It's the same meal he has every Sunday morning because that's all he knows how to cook. Mama told him years ago she wasn't about to get up before dawn on the Lord's day to cook him breakfast.

I sat across from him and watched as he glanced from his sermon notes to his Bible and back again. I loved Daddy's Bible. The cover was worn and smelled like a blend of leather, sweat, and Brillo soap. The pages were marked with notes and stained with finger-prints.

Daddy finally noticed me. He glanced up and nod-ded. "Morning."

"Morning," I said.

Daddy wasn't much of a talker on Sunday morn-ings. I figured he needed to save it up for the sermon and all the chatting he had to do after the service. I didn't mind. I wasn't much for talking on Sunday mornings, either. I walked to the counter and buttered a slice of bread.

I chewed slowly and thought how life might have

been different had I been born a boy. Getting into trouble might not have been such a problem, seeing how boys get away with more of that sort of thing. I was supposed to have been a boy. Daddy didn't even bother thinking up girl names, he was that sure. I don't know if he ever got over the shock when I came out a girl. I would've been called Joseph Lee Clawson, Jr., except Mama hollered after the doctor to write Josephine on the birth certificate.

There wasn't any chance of a boy baby coming after me, either. Something happened to Mama's insides when I was born that made it so she couldn't have any more babies. Mama said it was Daddy's prayers caused the Good Lord to let her live. His prayers must not have been strong enough to talk the Good Lord into making me a boy.

It wasn't until I was done eating my bread and finishing off the last sips of orange juice that Daddy closed his Bible and straightened his sermon notes. He fiddled with his tie for a minute, then smoothed his hair with the palm of his hand. Daddy always looked proper and polished on Sundays, just the way a preacher should look, save for the scar running from his temple to his jaw. He got it fighting the Nazis in the war. Daddy had a handsome face, but it was the scar I liked best.

Daddy looked me over. "Wear something new to church this morning, Josephine. Something pretty."

I nodded.

"And have your mama fix your hair."

I touched my hair, trying to smooth it straight. I could never make it look just right, but Mama had a way of combing the wild curls so they tucked under neat and respectable.

"Do you know your memory verse for Sunday school?"

"Yes, Daddy," I said, feeling my stomach clutch. Daddy had gotten my lesson in advance and made me learn it. It would have been much easier if I could have just remained ignorant and anonymous on the first day.

"What is it?"

"Daddy, I know it!"

"Well, what is it, then?"

I sighed and clenched my jaw. I was willing to bet no one else's father cared this much about a Sunday school memory verse.

"Esther 4:14," I said through tight teeth. "'And who knoweth whether thou art come to the kingdom for such a time as this?'"

"Do you know the first part of the verse?"

"We don't have to memorize that part, Daddy. Just the last bit."

"You should memorize the entire verse, Jo. It doesn't make sense out of context."

"Makes sense to me," I muttered.

"Good morning," Mama said. She stood in the doorway of the kitchen and smiled.

Daddy glanced at his watch, then stood to give Mama a kiss. "Morning, Maye," he said. "You look wonderful."

"Thank you," Mama said. She did look pretty. Her dark hair was combed into a twist at the nape of her neck, and she wore a blue velveteen dress that matched the color of her eyes. I glanced at her feet. They were bare. Mama hated wearing shoes and wouldn't put them on until the last possible moment.

"Maye!" Daddy stared at her feet. "What if somebody stops by and sees you?"

"Why, darling, I'll simply tell them I am standing on holy ground." She winked at Daddy, but he didn't smile. "You going over to the church?"

"Yes. Thought I'd go and make sure everything is ready. You'll be there soon?" He kept glancing at her feet and twitching his jaw.

"I'll be there."

"Jo, too." He glared at me. "Don't be late."

I'd never been late for church a day in my life, but before I could say anything, Mama clutched my arm. She held on to me as we watched Daddy walk out of the parsonage and across the street to the brick and pil-lared church.

"Don't pay him any mind, Jo," Mama said, finally letting go. "He's just nervous."

What did he have to be nervous about? I wondered. I was the one about to be marched into the lion's den. But I didn't say it out loud. Mama was pretty and polite with everyone. She wouldn't know what it was like try-ing to make new friends. We finished getting ready, then followed Daddy.

Brother Barnaby Baxter introduced us to the con-gregation during opening announcements. "This Sun-day, August the fourth of 1957, is an auspicious day in the life of this church. We are blessed with a new pastor and his family." Brother Baxter spoke in long, drawn-out tones, stuck in slow speed. I swallowed a yawn. "I am honored to introduce and welcome our new reverend, Joseph Clawson, who many of you know grew up right near here; his beautiful wife, Maye; and his daughter, Josephine." We all stood to polite applause. No one ever introduced me as beautiful, the way they did Mama. Mama said it was only because I hadn't grown into myself yet. I didn't mind. It was bad enough folks expecting me to be perfect because my daddy was the preacher. It'd be even worse if I was hung with the problem of being beautiful, too.

After announcements the kids marched down to the basement for Sunday school. My class was in a big cement room divided into smaller rooms by partitions. The sixth-grade partition was filled with rickety chairs, a cracked blackboard, and a fuzzy flannel picture of Jesus. It smelled like chalk and mildew, a smell I knew from other Sunday schools in other churches.

I chewed on the edge of my thumb, studying over the classroom. I chose a seat in the back row next to a boy wearing a starched white shirt that appeared to be choking him.

The teacher walked to the front of the class. "Children! Children!" she said, clapping. "Good morning, children."

"Good morning, Miss Hasty," everyone sang.

I scrunched down in my seat, hoping against hope that Miss Hasty would just get on with the lesson and mercifully ignore my presence in the back row. But it wasn't to be. What I couldn't figure out was if Sunday school teachers didn't know the impact they had on my life or if they just didn't care.

"We have a very special friend with us this morning," Miss Hasty said. "Our new reverend's little girl, Josephine. Welcome, Josephine." She clapped again vigorously, then made a great show of peering over the other kids to look for me. I prayed the floor might open and swallow me whole.

"Come on up to the front, Josephine. You don't need to be hiding out in the back. I'm sure you of all people have learned the Sunday school lesson and aren't shy about answering Bible questions."

I stood reluctantly and shuffled to the front of the class.

"Don't slouch, dear," Miss Hasty whispered.

Someone laughed. I felt my face flush.

Miss Hasty steered me to a seat front and center, next to a girl she called Bobby Sue Snyder. Bobby Sue looked me over. I smoothed my skirt and tried to smile. Bobby Sue just arched her eyebrows. She was wearing a quilted circle skirt of pink satin. The skirt looked so shimmery, I wanted to reach out and pet it. But I didn't. I chewed my thumb instead.

Miss Hasty pursed her lips and stared pointedly at my thumb. I snatched it out of my mouth and clutched my hands in my lap.

Miss Hasty drilled me with questions all morning. I felt obligated to answer every one so Daddy wouldn't be shamed on his first day. Then she praised my Bible knowledge and set it up as an example to the class.

"She's like a Bible encyclopedia," someone whispered.

I knew I would never live this down, no matter how many kids I clobbered. And I had already promised I wouldn't do any more fighting.

After class I trooped upstairs to church and huddled next to Mama in the wooden pew. We sang some and prayed some, then Daddy got up to preach. He had a glint in his eye, and his voice thundered across the sanctuary. In every town he'd ever preached, Daddy had found a cause to take on—be it gambling or smoking or cursing. He sure knew how to use his words to fight against the evil and the depraved. I wondered what kind of cause Daddy would find in Jericho. It seemed such a proper and sleepy-type place.

I didn't so much listen to Daddy's sermons as let them wash over me. His words resonated and flowed and made images come to life in my mind. Most of the time I didn't quite know what he was talking about, but I always came away with the thought of something—a dove or a cross or lakes of burning fire. That seemed to be enough to satisfy Daddy that I'd been paying attention when he quizzed me after church.

Today's sermon got me thinking about our new home at the parsonage. Not the faded chintz sofa that smelled like old ladies or the cracked vinyl kitchen chairs that made my legs sweat, but the good things. Things like the flowers Mama planted in front of the wraparound porch, and the white eyelet curtains in my room that fluttered in the breeze, and my very own bed with the blue star-burst quilt.

I could tell the other folks were liking it, too, because no one snored or let their head droop on the pew in front of them. They waved their fans provided by Moore's Funeral Parlor and nodded. At the end of the sermon everyone shouted, "Amen!" which for Baptists is a lot like applause.

"Hometown boy makes good," Mama whispered. I looked at Mama, then glanced up at Daddy's face as he looked over his new congregation. I had a sinking feeling in my stomach. It didn't look like Daddy would be getting a call from God to leave Jericho anytime soon, which meant I'd better figure out how to make some friends.

chapter two

We'd only been a week in Jericho when Mama hired
Mrs. Abilene Jefferson.

I'd never seen a colored person up close before.
They didn't live in places like Harrisburg, Indiana. I
once heard that a carful of colored boys stopped in
Harrisburg for gasoline on their way to Indianapolis. I
didn't get a chance to look at them, but Avery Phillips,
whose father owned the Flying K gas station, did. He
said the colored boys were listening to Bo Diddley on
the radio, drinking grape Nehi, and cutting up. Avery
sure made it sound like a big deal.

I was cleaning off breakfast dishes first thing Tuesday morning when I heard a knocking on the back
door. I rushed to answer it, then stood dumbfounded.

"Mama," I called, wanting to turn around and yell

for her but not wanting to take my eyes off the two visitors.

A Negro woman and a boy carrying a battered, green toolbox stood on the back porch. The woman smiled and nodded.

"Mama!" I yelled again.

I stared at them. They were both dark, chocolate colored.

I heard Mama bustle up behind me. She extended her hand. "Abilene," she said. "Welcome. So good to see you again. Please, come in."

The woman and the boy followed Mama inside. I scooted out of the way, my eyes still riveted on the two.

"This be my son, Lucas," Abilene said. "You said you got some plumbin' need fixin'?"

Mama gestured at the kitchen. "The kitchen sink has a leak. Why don't you check that first?"

Lucas nodded.

"This is my daughter, Josephine." Mama put a hand on my shoulder. My face grew warm.

I heard a loud pounding. Daddy was outside patching up leaks in the parsonage roof. Some folks thought preachers only worked on Sundays, but that wasn't true of Daddy.

"Abilene, would you please start in the living room?

Everything you'll need is in the cupboard next to the sink. I'll be in my room getting ready if you have any questions."

I stared at Mama. She didn't return my look, just walked out of the kitchen and into her room. She began brushing her hair. I followed her, looking back over my shoulder and trying to see what Abilene and Lucas were doing.

"Stop gawking, Jo," Mama said.

"But Mama," I protested. "What are they *doing* here?"

"Peddling bottles of Magic Jim's Cure-All Formula?" Mama said dryly.

"Mama!"

"It appears they are cleaning and looking over the plumbing."

That answer wasn't much better. I could see *that's* what they were doing.

There was more banging from outside. It sounded like Daddy was trying to drive the hammer through the ceiling.

"But why? Why are they here? Why is that colored woman messing about our house?"

Mama's eyes flashed. I took a step back. "Her name is Mrs. Jefferson, and I expect you to treat her as you would any adult." She glared at me, then put down her brush and began coating her lips with a pale pink gloss. "Mrs. Jefferson will be doing some cleaning and cooking for us," she said once she finished her lips.

"Yes, but Mama . . ."

"And I don't want you giving her any sass. She asks you to do something and you do it."

My head was starting to whirl. That woman was our *maid*! "Does Daddy know?"

Mama's lips pursed. "Of course," she said shortly. Outside there was a clatter, then a series of sharp blows.

"I still don't understand. . . ." A thought flashed into my head. "Are we rich?" Only folks I'd ever known to have a maid were rich folks. I'd never known *anybody* who had a colored maid.

Mama frowned. She sat on the edge of her bed, then patted the spot next to her. I climbed up.

"I should've told you before, but everything's been happening so fast. I was offered a job at Treva Lane's dress shop downtown. I'll be working there several days a week."

My head spun like I'd been hit with a sharp right hook. "You got a job?"

Some days I couldn't figure Mama out. Just when I got to thinking she was a regular and normal-type mother, she'd do something that knocked that idea on its head. Like the time in Indiana she got Daddy's .22 and killed a weasel that was messing with the chickens. She was a dead-on shot, but I'd never seen her pick up a gun before or since.

And now this. Regular mothers didn't get jobs. Folks were going to say Daddy couldn't support us or that Mama was acting below her station. I couldn't believe Daddy had agreed to this. But then, once Mama got her mind set on something, no one, not even Daddy, could change it. Daddy said Mama was as stubborn as a mule and had opinions about things most folks never even thought about. He said it was because she grew up surrounded by Indians and mountains and books by people like Thomas Paine and John Milton and Harriet Beecher Stowe.

Another loud series of bangs echoed from outside into the house.

"You're a big girl now, Jo. You don't need me home so much. I want to do this."

"But what about Mrs. Jefferson . . . ?"

"I met Abilene when I was out visiting. Her daddy knew about your daddy when he was a little boy. Isn't that something?"

One thing about Mama, she took the commandment to love thy neighbor seriously. She went visiting once or twice a week. It didn't take long before she'd know nearly everything about everyone. Folks opened right up to her. Told her their whole life story, sometimes. I went with her every now and then, but hearing about other folks' aches and pains made my head hurt. I was like Daddy in that way.

"Abilene's a widow and needs the money. She can keep things running around here three days a week while I'm at the shop. It seems to have worked itself out perfectly, don't you think?"

I shrugged. I didn't know what to say.

Mama stood like everything was settled and gave me a kiss on my forehead. "You be a good girl and do what Abilene tells you. Daddy will be working on the roof all day if you need him."

It took a moment for it to sink in, but once it did, I stood with a yelp. "You're leaving?"

"I'm going to work."

"Today? Already? Just like that?" My heart seemed to flip in my chest. "But Mama, what am I going to do about them?" I said the last part in a whisper.

Mama bent down and looked fearfully about. "About whom?"

"Them," I said, pointing to the other room with my eyes. "The Negroes."

Mama stood. "For heaven's sake, Jo," she said, flicking her white gloves at me. "Don't be so dramatic. They're people, just like everyone else. Now have a good day. I'll be home by four."

I watched in mute horror as Mama walked into the family room and said something to Abilene. Then Lucas walked up and stood next to his mama. He set the toolbox on the floor. Abilene nudged him.

"Ma'am," he said. "I looked over your plumbin' an' found a couple things." He stared at the baseboards while he talked.

"Yes?" Mama said. Lucas continued.

"Gasket in the kitchen plumb wore out an' the slip nuts were loose," he said. "That's all, there. Liftin' wire in the bathroom needed tightenin', an' I fixed the snubber in the washin' machine. Everything else okay."

He sounded like he knew what he was talking about, but I didn't believe it. He couldn't be much older than me. What did he know about plumbing?

Mama smiled. "Thank you for your work," she said. She reached into her purse, then handed two dollars to Lucas. I watched the money change hands with wide eyes. Lucas took the money gingerly, as if Mama might snatch it back, then he studied it and grinned wide.

"Thank you, ma'am!" he said. He shoved the money

in his pocket and looked at his mama. She nodded, so he took off running to the door and on out. He ran in a funny kind of gallop, making the tools in his toolbox clank up and down. I couldn't tell if he was excited or if that was his regular way.

Then Mama breezed out the door, and suddenly it was just me and Abilene alone in the house. I strained my ears for the sound of Daddy and was relieved when I heard another clatter and a string of words that Daddy used in place of swearing.

I hung back, chewing on the edge of my thumb and thinking what I was to do. If Abilene noticed me, she didn't say. She just hummed to herself as she polished the sideboard. She had wide, full lips dark as berries and a high forehead that furrowed while she hummed. I wondered what she'd find to do for three days a week. The parsonage wasn't a big house, and I'd bet money that Daddy wouldn't let me out of doing chores. But maybe it did take all that time to keep a house clean, at least in South Carolina. Mama complained something fierce about the Carolina clay that stained everything a brick red. She scrubbed the front porch steps for an hour before declaring it would take God's own miracle to get them white again. Perhaps she meant Abilene to take care of those red steps.

"We've never had anybody come in to clean our house," I said finally.

"I 'spect it'll take some gettin' used to," she said. Her voice flowed warm and slow.

"Do you clean a lot of folks' houses, Mrs. Jefferson?" I perched on the edge of the sofa and put my thumb under my armpit. I'd chewed it raw, and it stung like bees.

She chuckled, a deep sound that came from her belly. "You be callin' me Mrs. Jefferson? Ain't no need for that. Mrs. Jefferson's my mother-in-law, heaven rest her soul." She shook her head. "That was some kind of harsh woman, all angles and jutting bones she was. Sharp mouth, too, land's sakes. I be scared to death of her the first five years of my marriage. Now if anyone says Mrs. Jefferson, I think she be standing right behind me ready to holler I ain't done the corn bread right."

I smiled, then remembered something and frowned. "But Mama says I'm to call you Mrs. Jefferson. I don't see how that'd be respectful if it made you jumpy every time I said it."

"No, don't reckon it would. Maybe your mama'd let us meet somewhere in the middle, an' you can call me Miz Abilene."

I nodded. It sounded a bit like music, the way she said it. "I don't think she'd mind. That's how I call most white grown women, less'n they're the starchy type or a teacher."

Miz Abilene raised an eyebrow at me. She straightened and surveyed the room. "Your mama done a good job makin' this place homey." She looked me over. "You help her some?"

"Yes, ma'am. I got lots of chores, on account of I'm the only child. You have other children, Miz Abilene?"

"I got three. Simon is near seventeen. Lucas is twelve, and LouEllen, my baby, be eight."

"I'm eleven," I announced, thinking Abilene wasn't so hard to talk to after all. She had an easy way about her, but her eyes were sharp and quick. "Do they all do plumbing? Or just Lucas? How'd he learn it?"

"Their pa taught 'em, heaven rest his soul. They all do what work they can get. Don't matter just what."

"Even LouEllen? She works, too?" I wondered what it would feel like to have a job where folks passed you money. I guessed it'd be fun. Maybe that's why Mama was doing it.

"Shore. She's pickin' fruit an' cotton some days an' runnin' errands an' such. Everybody gotta help somehow." Her jaw twitched. "Ain't easy. Never easy." Her eyes grew dark.

"What do you mean?" I asked, but my question was interrupted by a banging at the window.

"Look there," Abilene said. A bird fluttered against the window, staring in with darting eyes, then turned and flew back to a nest in the crook of our tree. "Now, what you know 'bout that! Y'all got a mockingbird in the neighborhood. Him flutterin' against the window thataway means he's trying to bring good luck." Abilene clucked her tongue. "Y'all never be lost for song with that one about. Think you got a treeful of birds the way they carry on. Mimics, they are." She reached over and put her hand on the window. "Don't let him in, though. Wild birds caught inside don't bring nothin' but trouble. They struggle too hard for freedom."

I stared out the window. The mockingbird cocked his head, then flew to a branch and began to sing. *Wheedle, wheedle, wheedle, teer.*

"See there? That's a wren song. Copy!" Abilene turned and went back to polishing the sideboard. I watched the bird for a few minutes and listened while he sang. Then I tagged along after Abilene.

Before I knew it, the day was half done and Daddy thundered in for lunch. I was eating in the kitchen with Miz Abilene.

"Josephine!" Daddy hollered. "Finish your eating and come outside. I need you to pick up the roofing nails."

I nodded quickly. I wasn't about to argue with Daddy when he used that voice. I gulped my lunch and rinsed my plate in the sink.

Abilene set a plate of fried corn bread and greens in front of Daddy. He stared at it before stabbing a forkful and shoving it into his mouth. He never said a word to Miz Abilene.

chapter three

I'd been in Jericho for more than a week, but I wasn't making much headway toward finding friends. I had approached a group of boys who were playing stickball in the sandlot by the school, but they just laughed and told me girls couldn't play. It was the same in every town I'd ever lived. So I spent my days with Abilene. She taught me how to brew a nettle tea that would straighten my hair and told me what to eat to keep from getting sunstroke.

Most mornings I woke to the mockingbird, singing away at some other bird's song, but Friday morning I woke to the sound of Daddy arguing with Mama.

". . . have to drive to Greenville today," I heard him say. "I won't be around to keep an eye on Jo. I don't want her spending the whole day with Abilene."

"Whyever not?" Mama asked. Her voice had an edge to it that made me shiver. I swung out of bed and tiptoed toward the door.

"You said you'd only be working three days a week. Today makes it four. What's next? You haven't spent any time with Jo as it is!"

Mama had told me last night that she wanted to go into the dress shop this morning to help Treva sort through new fabric and that she'd be back by lunch. I told her I didn't mind. Daddy sure seemed mad, though.

"Is that what this is about?" Mama asked, her voice still tight and cold. "How much time I spend with Jo?"

"You're her mother!" Daddy blustered. "She shouldn't be pestering Abilene. You hired a maid, not a wet nurse!"

"Fine," Mama said, but her voice was still sharp.

I waited all through breakfast for Mama to say something to me about how I was to spend my day, but she never did. I didn't, either. I didn't want her to know I'd been eavesdropping. At eight o'clock Abilene arrived on the back porch. Mama spoke to her, then kissed me on the cheek and told me to have a good day.

"You go and get youself somethin' to do," Miz Abilene said after I'd helped her with the breakfast dishes. "Out from underfoot."

"Nothing to do," I said, wondering what Mama had said to her. "Don't have any friends yet, and the library's closed until the librarian gets back from visiting her sister in Atlanta." I hated the library being closed and not having something to read. Moving from church to church like we did made it hard to keep friends, but I never had to worry about losing the company of books.

"Make your own fun, then. Go outside."

"Too hot."

"Go swimming."

I scowled. I'd heard the kids in my Sunday school class talk about swimming at the country club pool, but no one invited me, and I wasn't a member. "Nowhere to swim," I said.

Abilene nodded. "I done swum in the river when I was a girl," she said. "But don't reckon you should be doing that."

"Why not?"

Abilene shrugged. "Ain't fitting. Not for the likes of you."

I felt a surge of excitement. "It ain't?" I imagined the river, cool and dark and secret, where no one would be watching 'cause they wouldn't think to look for me there.

"Reckon you're right," I said. "Maybe I'll just go outside, then. Bye!"

I raced to my room to grab my bathing suit and towel, then tried to sneak out the back door. Abilene met me. She didn't say anything, just handed me an onion. Said eating it would keep me cool. I munched it while I walked down Plantation Drive. All it did was make my eyes water and my mouth burn. I tossed the onion, then came to the place where the road forked at the Keonee County Farm and Fleet. The right-hand fork curved past the lacy beech and elm trees that graced the front of the Snyders' pillared mansion, then meandered into downtown Jericho. That's the road Mama walked to work. The left-hand fork plunged into a scrubby grove of oak and pine, past a board fence with rusted wire on top. The river was just beyond the fence, but I'd not explored that far. That was where the colored folks lived, on the other side of that fence.

The day shimmered in the sun, hot as a slow stew, but a shiver ran through me at the thought of crossing the fence. It wasn't fitting. That's what Daddy had said, and Abilene, too. I stood at the fork in the road, unsure. A sawmill truck rumbled past, carrying stacks of logs harvested back in the hills. It smelled of raw wood and diesel. Red mud clung to its tires. The truck passed. I heard the birds singing in the tall trees and felt the wind breeze past, carrying the scent of river. I took a deep breath.

I ran through the meadow behind the Farm and Fleet, then plunged into the woods alongside the fence. The trees were so tall, I could barely see their tops. The ground was littered with leaves and needles. I inhaled the smell of pine and decay.

The fence was as tall as my chest, with thick posts and mean stretches of barbed wire. It seemed to extend forever. I followed it through the woods. I stayed on the white side, eyeing the vicious barbs lining the top. *Shoot,* I thought, *I ain't scared.* I knew Miz Abilene, and she wasn't nothing to fear. I found a section with no barbed wire, and before I could think too much, I climbed over to the other side.

The river flowed rich and muddy. It cut through red clay banks lined with trees that leaned into the water. I poked along the bank until it leveled and the river widened and pooled. A tree had fallen and extended into the water. I looked around to be sure no one was watching, then stripped off my clothes and pulled on my bathing suit.

I scrambled across the log, poked a stick into the

water to make sure there were no snakes lurking about, then jumped in.

The water closed over me, silty and smooth. My toes sank into the muddy bottom, and I pushed back to the surface. It was deep, nearly to my shoulders. I ducked up and down, trying to grab fish with my hands. Then I floated on my back, staring into the deep blue sky.

I climbed onto the log and gazed around. The river had churned mud red with my kicking. A soft wind whispered in the trees, and invisible birds chirped and sang. I had the feeling I was the only person in the world, that God had made this place just for me. Something bubbled up in me, something good and fresh. I jumped off the log and skipped through the trees, feeling the warm earth under my bare feet and the sun on my river-washed skin.

I closed my eyes, tilted my head to the sky, and grinned.

Smack! I plowed into something solid and fell backward with a thud.

When I opened my eyes, I saw a Negro boy sitting on his backside, looking stunned. A big yellow dog sat next to him. It showed its teeth to me, then looked at the boy and whimpered.

"Why don't you watch where you're going?" I said,

because I couldn't think of anything else to say and because I was a little scared and embarrassed.

"I wasn't goin' nowhere," he said. "I was just standin' here. You the one runnin' like a crazy person."

"I was not running like a crazy—hey, you're the boy who fixed our sink. Miz Abilene's boy, Lucas."

"That's right." He stood and brushed himself off.

I stood, too. I looked Lucas up and down. He was taller than me, with short black hair and eyes the color of toffee. His dog let out a low whine. I told myself I wasn't a bit scared, but my heart was hammering so, I couldn't think. Words just blurted out of my mouth.

"Your mama's our maid."

He stiffened. "So?"

"So, nothing. I'm just saying."

He snorted and turned up his nose like he smelled something nasty.

"What was that for?" I asked.

"Nothin'." He smiled, but it didn't reach his eyes. His dog barked and wagged his tail. I reached out a hand to let him sniff it. He licked my hand, then moved his head under it so I would pet him. I laughed.

"What's your dog's name?"

Lucas glared at his dog. "Moses," he said, more to the dog than to me. "Come on, boy."

"That's a strange name. Why do you call him Moses?"

Lucas gave a sigh, but his eyes sparkled just a bit. "On account of one day I was just walkin' along when down the river floated this ole, wooden tub. I figured Ma could use the tub for somethin', so I swum after it. I grabbed the tub and dragged it to shore. When I looked inside, there was this puppy all wet and shiverin', half dead from hunger and a leg all broke."

"How'd he get in there?"

"Litter of pups musta got dumped in the river. This one here got away somehow."

"Who would do such a thing?" I asked, patting Moses's head. "Dump a litter of puppies? That's awful!"

He rolled his eyes. "Happens," he said. "Lotsa mean folks around."

"Good thing you found him," I said, and ruffled Moses's ears. I looked Moses over and couldn't find a thing on him to show he'd nearly died. "Did you patch him up?"

"Yep." Lucas's face softened. "I splinted his leg and fed him good. He hopped about on three legs for a long time, but now he's like new. Ain't ya, boy?" Lucas ruffled his dog's head. Our hands brushed. We both pulled away like we'd touched a hot cinder.

"You come out to these woods a lot?" I asked. I put my hands behind my back.

Lucas stiffened again. "I'm just on my way home."

"It's my first time seeing this part of the river. Sure is pretty," I said.

"White folks got a piece of river, too," he said. "Upstream. In town."

"I know." The river acted more tame as it flowed through the city of Jericho, slowly meandering past a grassy park and under a concrete bridge. It didn't seem the same river. This one, burbling through the shady woods, felt more real somehow.

"You live in the colored quarters?" I asked.

"Ain't you bright," he muttered.

I glared at him and thought about knocking him down. But he was bigger than me, and I'd made my promise not to fight.

"I was just trying to be polite," I said with as much courtesy as I could muster. "Leastways your dog isn't rude." Moses leaned heavy against my leg.

"You're a strange one," Lucas said, looking me over. "Reckon it's on account of your being a Yankee. Simon says Yankees got strange ways 'cause it's so cold up North."

I took offense at that. "I am not strange, and you

don't know nothin' 'bout Yankees. You take that back!"
I stared at him with my fist clenched.

Lucas shook his head. "I ain't takin' it back. Look at
how you're dressed."

I suddenly realized I was still in my bathing suit. I
wrapped my arms around my chest and grimaced.

"Why you swimmin' in the river 'stead of at the
swimmin' pool?" he asked.

"None of your business," I said.

He shrugged. "Best let no one catch you." He patted
his leg, jolting Moses from his semiconscious daze.
"Come on, boy. Let's git. Say good-bye to strange,
Yankee Jo." Moses licked my hand, then looked at
Lucas. They started through the woods. Lucas walked
with a limp that made him lurch up and over.

"Hey!" I called after him.

He stopped and turned to look at me. "Why do you
walk like that?" I asked.

He frowned. "That ain't none of *your* business," he
said.

I shrugged like I didn't care, but I stood and watched
as Lucas bobbed through the woods, following the
fence. Then he and Moses disappeared into the colored
quarters.

chapter four

The library finally opened on Monday. I'd survived another Sunday in Jericho and was glad to get it behind me. Right after lunch I raced to town. The sheriff was sweeping the front steps of the jail. He was the tidiest sheriff I'd ever seen, always sweeping or polishing or tweaking his uniform. He had a pocket packed tight with peppermints. I waved. He stopped sweeping and waved back. Then I climbed the steps of the town hall to the room that held the library.

"You must be Josephine," the librarian said when I walked to the lending desk.

"Yes, ma'am." I was used to strangers knowing who I was.

"I'm Miss Spinnaker. I'm a founding member of First Baptist Church of Jericho. I remember your father when he was just knee-high to a grasshopper."

"Yes'm. May I have a library card, please?" Miss Spinnaker was old, with stiff, white hair and spectacles. She had that smell of Listerine and lilac talcum worn by most proper old ladies.

"Of course, dear, I'm just getting to that. Your daddy surely did apply himself, didn't he? What with him starting out the way he did."

"Yes'm." Mama told me how Daddy had lived in a poor run-down shack in the hills, but Daddy never said a word about it. It was hard to imagine him being a little boy, and poor.

"I was right surprised when your father elected to apply for this pastorate, him having spent so much time up North. We thought maybe he'd forgotten us after winning those medals in the war."

"No'm."

"I don't believe I know your mother. Where are her people from?"

"Tennessee, mostly." Mama was from that part of Appalachia that refused to secede from the Union during the Civil War. I didn't say that to Miss Spinnaker. I also didn't tell her that Mama's grandmother had been pure Cherokee and had heard the stories about the Trail of Tears. Most folks regarded that as a bit odd. Even Daddy. I found it exciting. I guessed that's why Mama cared so much about the sick and broken down.

"Tennessee? How did she meet your father?"

"I'm not sure." I crossed my fingers behind my back as I told the lie. Mama and Daddy met at a dance during the war, but I couldn't tell her that. Proper Baptist folks like Miss Spinnaker didn't abide by dancing, war or no war.

"I wondered if I might check out some books?"

"Certainly." She passed across a card. "Please, no talking in the library."

"Yes'm."

I took the card. The Jericho library was a peaceful, drowsy kind of place. I moved carefully. Library noises always sounded hushed and muffled, like prayers in a church. Sometimes I wondered if maybe God didn't live in libraries, too.

I scanned through the titles and pulled books until I had a stack. I carried them to the desk and set them down along with my card.

"Why, Josephine, the limit is four books at a time to children," Miss Spinnaker said. "You'll need to put two back."

"Only four?"

"Those are the rules, dear."

She indicated a sign listing library policies. I sighed and studied my stack.

I hung on to *The Adventures of Huckleberry Finn*, which I had started to read in Indiana but couldn't finish because we moved, and some Judy Bolton mysteries, which I thought quite grown up.

"Those are due in two weeks," Miss Spinnaker said.

"Don't worry. I'll have 'em done by then." I grabbed the books and raced outside.

Abilene didn't care what I did with my time, so long as I was home by dinner. I wandered down Main Street, looking in store windows and kicking rocks. If I got 'em just right, they skedaddled straight down the sidewalk and I could kick 'em again once I caught up.

I was midkick at the drugstore when I looked in the picture window and saw the girls from my Sunday school class sitting at the soda counter and giggling. A pang of loneliness shot through me.

Before I could think myself out of it, I pulled open the door and walked on through the drugstore to the soda counter. I clutched my books under my arm.

"Hey," I said casually.

"Hey," answered Bobby Sue Snyder. She was wearing embroidered capri pants and saddle shoes. I felt suddenly silly in my boxy homemade shorts stained with red clay.

"What can I get for you?" The soda jerk stared at me impatiently.

I shrugged, knowing I didn't have a dime in my pocket. "I'm still deciding," I said.

He rolled his eyes. "Let me know, then." He walked away and started wiping down the soda fountain.

The girls went back to talking among themselves and ignoring me. I wandered over to the jukebox and pretended to study it.

"Maybe I'll play Elvis," I said out loud.

The girls stopped talking and looked at me. "You listen to Elvis?" Bobby Sue asked.

The lie was out of my mouth before I could stop it. "Sure. I've even got his records."

"Lucky." Martha Pierson sighed. "My dad's such a square. I can listen to Elvis on the radio, but he won't let me buy any records."

"My dad doesn't care."

"Really?"

Every eye was on me now. I smiled and shrugged like it was no big deal. My stomach clenched a little, but at least they wouldn't think I was the Goody Two-shoes Miss Hasty made me seem in Sunday school.

"Maybe you could come over and we could listen to your records on my daddy's record player," Bobby Sue said.

"Sure." I grinned, forgetting for a moment that I had no records. "That'd be fun."

Bobby Sue took a last slurp from her soda, then hopped off the stool. The other girls followed her lead. "I'm going to Harper's Five and Ten," she said. She looked at me. "Want to come?"

"Okay." My heart leapt. I followed the girls outside.

"Ooh, look who it is," Bobby Sue said, pointing.

I looked and saw a thin woman pulling a rusty wagon that was piled high with baskets. A little girl walked alongside her.

"Who?"

The girls all looked at me with wide eyes, like they couldn't believe I didn't know.

"It's Lenore Cooper," Katie Moore said finally. "She's bad. Really bad."

"What did she do?"

The girls looked at the ground and smirked. Bobby Sue finally answered.

"See that little girl? She's mixed."

"Mixed?"

"Her daddy was mulatto. A half Negro." Bobby Sue said the last word in a whisper.

I stared at the woman and her daughter in fascination. "Do they live in the Quarters?"

"No. Colored folks don't want them either. *She* lives back in the hills," Bobby Sue said knowingly. "Hides out. *He* got run out of town. To protect Southern womanhood, you know. Come on, let's go to Harper's before she comes this way."

I wasn't sure what southern womanhood was or why it needed protecting, but I followed them across the street to the five-and-ten. Lenore Cooper stopped in front of Treva Lane's dress shop. I saw Mama come out of the store.

"Look! Isn't that your mother?" one of the girls asked.

"She's talking to Lenore Cooper!"

I felt hot with embarrassment. "Come on. Let's go to Harper's," I mumbled. I should have known Mama would get caught talking to someone like Lenore Cooper.

I rushed inside the five-and-ten. The girls stopped to look through a fashion magazine. My eye caught the latest *Adventure* comic. I longed to flip through it, but I stopped myself. The girls wandered to the makeup counter.

I tried to look interested as they talked about the few times their mothers let them wear nail polish and whether or not they'd be allowed to wear it to school this year. I saw a drinking fountain along the wall and realized how thirsty I was. I broke away from the group and walked toward it. I shifted my books to my chest, then leaned over to get a drink.

A hand grabbed my arm. I jumped, and my books clattered to the floor. Water dripped down my chin.

"What . . . ?" I began.

"What are you doing?" Bobby Sue stared at me, looking shocked. Girls surrounded her, and they all were looking at me the same way.

"Getting a drink of water," I said. "What's wrong?"

She stuck out her tongue. "That's disgusting."

"What is?" I was starting to feel panicked. I looked around, wondering what I'd done. A few adults glanced our way. "What?"

"Can't you read?" Bobby Sue asked. She pointed to a sign over the drinking fountain.

"Course I can!" I looked up and read the crudely lettered sign: Colored. Then I glanced to my right and saw another drinking fountain with a sign that said White Only. My eyes widened, and my chest squeezed tight.

"I didn't see the sign," I tried to explain. My mouth tasted funny, and I felt tears prick the back of my eyes. "I didn't know. I didn't see. . . ."

Bobby Sue wrinkled her nose. A couple of the girls giggled behind their hands.

"I didn't see. . . ." I choked on the words when I realized they all were laughing at me. I grabbed my books and ran blindly out the door. I didn't stop running until I reached the safety of my room.

❧

I spent the rest of the afternoon huddled on my bed. My stomach grumbled with hunger. I was beginning to wonder if anyone even noticed I was gone when Mama knocked on my door.

"Jo. Time for dinner."

"I'm not hungry."

She opened the door and peeked in. "May I come in?" she asked.

I shrugged and stared at the ceiling. "Don't care." I was starting to ache from lying still so long.

Mama walked over and sat on the edge of the bed. "Abilene said you've been in here all afternoon. That's not like you. What's wrong?"

I shrugged, trying to make it seem like nothing, but my lower lip quivered.

Mama brushed a strand of hair off my face and tucked it behind my ear. Her hand felt cool and smelled like jasmine. The words bubbled out of me.

"Oh, Mama. I drank out of the colored water fountain and I didn't know and everybody laughed at me and I wanted the girls to like me but now they all think I'm stupid and disgusting. I hate it here; why can't we go back to Indiana?" My voice cracked with tears.

"You drank . . ." Mama looked at me, and I could see her trying to sort it all out. Her eyes flashed with anger, and for a minute I thought she'd think me stupid, too. Then her eyes softened.

"Oh, honey, it's okay." Mama stroked my hair. "It was an honest mistake."

"It's *not* okay. They laughed at me!"

"In a few days everyone will forget all about it."

I shook my head. I wanted to believe that was true, but I knew down deep that it wasn't.

"Oh, Jo, I'm sorry. But it will all blow over, I promise. It was, well, it was kind of like you pulled the bathroom door closed."

"What?"

Mama smiled. "When I was sixteen, just after my daddy died, I went to Atlanta to spend the summer with my great-aunt Rose. She was frightfully sophisticated, at least to my mind. The first Sunday I was there, we entertained. I tried so hard to impress all those elegant southern women, but by the end of the afternoon they were casting scornful glances my way and rushing to get home. I didn't know what I'd done wrong. Turns out I had closed the bathroom door. How could I have known that was dreadfully rude, that proper folks wouldn't dare knock on a closed bathroom door to see if it was empty? Hers was the first house I'd ever visited with indoor plumbing. All I knew were outhouses, and you sure didn't want those doors open. Aunt Rose looked at me like I was plain white trash. She didn't entertain again, the whole summer I was there. I was so humiliated. For years after I couldn't pass an indoor bathroom without my cheeks burning with shame."

"Oh, Mama. That's not the same."

Mama twisted a strand of my hair around her finger. "I wanted so much to impress those women. They just scorned me. I learned something, though."

"What, Mama? To leave the bathroom door open?"

Mama laughed. "I learned that looking like a fool only smarts for a little while and that true friends will like you for who you are, silly mistakes and all."

"But, Mama . . ." I shook my head and swiped my eyes with the back of my hand. Those girls would never like me now. I was a laughingstock. Mama couldn't understand how it felt. She was a grown-up. Grown-ups didn't have to worry about making friends.

Daddy was sitting at the kitchen table waiting for dinner when I finally emerged from my room. I slid into my chair. Daddy looked at Mama, then at me. "Ready to eat now?"

I nodded, not wanting to tell him what had happened. He'd hear about it eventually, from someone. There were always folks around ready to tell the preacher on me.

Daddy said grace, and we started to eat. After a bit, Mama cleared her throat.

"I invited a woman to church today," she said. "Someone I met while visiting."

"Wonderful," Daddy said. "Always good to see a new face."

Daddy was always saying things like that, but we were usually the only new faces in a church. Everybody else had been around years and years.

"She has a daughter. Two years old."

"She can go to the nursery."

"The nursery workers won't take her."

That made Daddy pause in his eating. He looked at Mama. I looked at her, too. "Whyever not?" he asked.

"Because it's Lenore Cooper's little girl."

"Oh." Daddy's face paled. "Well. Maybe she ought to find another church, then . . ."

"Whatever do you mean, Joseph?" Mama asked. I tensed. Those were Mama's fighting words. *Whatever do you mean, Jo, by throwing slugs in Brother Ed's pumpkin patch? I think you best weed his garden as an apology. I* thought Daddy ought to cut out quick. I could tell he thought so, too. His eyes jerked this way and that, like a rabbit caught in a trap.

"She lives so far . . . other churches closer . . . doesn't have a car . . ."

Mama raised her eyebrows. I knew that look. I sat back in my seat, out of the way.

"Maye, listen, we've talked about this. Folks around here are just not ready for that kind of . . . for that kind of familiarity."

"Is the church *white only,* too, along with everything else?" Mama asked with those eyebrows still raised.

I flinched, thinking of the water fountain.

"Don't be ridiculous!" Daddy's voice was raised. "It's just not that easy. You want folks thinking their preacher is some sort of, well, some sort of communist, stirring up ideas?" Daddy stared at his plate and attacked his green beans. I looked from Mama to Daddy before taking another bite of biscuit. Something going on between them, something sharp and tense. I didn't know what it was, but it set my teeth on edge.

chapter five

Mama was wrong. She said folks would forget about what I'd done, but they didn't. It had been nearly a week, and kids still pointed and laughed when they saw me. In class on Sunday, I raised my hand to ask Miss Hasty if I could be excused to the bathroom. On my way out Katie Moore whispered, "The colored facilities are out back." Everyone around her, including Bobby Sue, cracked up laughing.

I showed 'em, though. When I was done in the rest room, I not only pulled the door closed, I locked it. All through the final hymn I grinned as folks wiggled and danced in their seats, until Mama nudged me and asked what was so funny.

Even worse than being laughed at, though, was what was going on between Mama and Daddy. Daddy preached a sermon on Sunday that denounced the evils of drink. Folks seemed right pleased with that sermon. They were amening and nodding all over the place. Seemed to me he'd found his cause to fight. But after church, when Daddy asked Mama what she thought, she gave a little snort.

"Mighty interesting battle to pick," Mama said. "Considering this is a dry county."

"There are moonshiners in those hills," Daddy said. "And that's not only a sin against God, it's a sin against the state."

"If you were preaching in the hills, you'd have a fight on your hands," Mama said. "But down here, in Jericho, only thing folks are drinking is their grandmother's peach cordial."

"Everyone else seemed to like it," Daddy said. "Attendance is up, and offerings, too."

"Well, as long as folks are happy." Mama's words had an edge to them. Then she raised those eyebrows and Daddy glared. The Sunday meal grew mighty quiet. I almost wished we had invited a couple of old ladies to dinner just to add to the conversation.

I spent most of my free time by the river. It was quiet there. The only person I ever saw was Lucas and his dog. He always paused to ask me what I was doing, but he stopped sounding rude about it. And he let me pat Moses.

After lunch on Tuesday, I struck out for the woods with *The Adventures of Huckleberry Finn* and a thermos full of sweet tea. Abilene said if I wouldn't eat an onion before I went out in the heat, then I'd better take some tea to quench my thirst. I didn't argue. Nobody made sweet tea like Abilene, not even Mama.

Walking outside was like getting slammed in the face with a wave of boiling air. It was so hot, the hound dogs at the Farm and Fleet couldn't do anything but flop under the porch with their tongues lolling out. I shuffled through the woods to the river, then stripped down to my bathing suit.

I jumped in. The water closed over me like a warm hug. I swam downstream until I was stopped by the sound of voices. I peeked out of the water, half hidden by leaves. Half a dozen colored boys were laughing and splashing in the river. I gasped, embarrassed on account of some of them had forgotten their bathing trunks. I ducked my head under, hoping I hadn't been seen. This must be their swimming hole. I swam back upstream, against the current, underwater most of the way.

When I got back to my spot, I dried off and pulled on my clothes, an old, ratty skirt and a T-shirt. The skirt made my legs feel cooler, and it was old enough it didn't matter if I got it dirty. Then I clambered onto the log to read about Huckleberry Finn. He spent most of his days on the river, having grand adventures. It made me wish I could have an adventure, too.

I was just to the part where Huck and Jim miss Cairo in the fog when something big and yellow hurtled toward me through the woods.

I nearly fell off my log into the river, book and all. Then I saw it was just Moses. He sort of tiptoed onto the log, then flopped down next to me to get a pat. He was panting and drooling all over my leg.

"You again," Lucas said when he got close. "You're always here."

"I ain't always here. Besides, it's a free country. I'm allowed to be here if I want." I didn't know if I was allowed, really, seeing as how I was on the colored side of the fence. But I didn't mention that.

He shrugged. "I reckon." He leaned down and cupped some water in his hands. "Shore is hot," he said, splashing his face.

"Sure is," I said. "I took a swim before. That cooled me off."

Lucas looked at me and laughed. "Ha! Girls can't swim."

"Can so!" I stood up, hands on my hips. "I can swim better than you, I'll bet."

"Can't neither." He rolled his eyes and shook his head.

I jumped off the log, put *Huckleberry Finn* with my thermos and towel, and charged toward him. "Want to bet? I bet I can swim to the other side of this river and back faster than you."

"You can't!" His eyes flashed. " 'Sides, you ain't s'posed to bet. Your daddy's the preacher."

"Pshaw," I said. "You're just chicken." Nobody was going to tell me I couldn't swim.

"I ain't chicken. I could beat you in a minute, just I ain't got no swim trunks."

I flushed, remembering those boys at the swimming hole. "Wear your clothes, then. Less'n you're chicken. Brawk, brawk." I flapped my arms. Moses barked, then jumped off the log into the river, splashing water every-where. "See. Even your dog thinks you're chicken."

"I ain't!" Lucas declared angrily.

"Race me, then."

"Shore, I will! But you gotta wear your clothes, too. No swimsuit."

"Fine. I don't care." I'd never swum in a skirt before, and I wondered how it would go. Still, a bet was a bet.

And I wasn't about to change back into my bathing suit with Lucas watching.

"No shoes, though." I looked down at Lucas's cracked and fraying boots. He frowned, then pulled off his boots and socks. One foot came out looking normal, but the other foot was crumpled and bent, without any toes.

"What happened to your foot?" I looked up at him. "Does it hurt?"

"Naw." He scowled. "I was born that way."

"That's why you walk the way you do," I said, feeling a surge of guilt. "You could have just told me. We don't have to race. I won't call you chicken."

"I can swim just as good as you, no matter 'bout my foot. You made a bet, an' you better keep it!"

"Fine! I will!" I forgot about his foot and pointed to the other side of the river. One tree etched white against the browns and greens of the others. "See that sycamore? We got to swim across the river, climb out, touch that tree, then swim back. First one to this side wins."

"All right." Lucas took a ready stance.

I bit my lip, wondering what I'd gotten myself into.

"On your mark, get set, GO!" I hollered.

I splashed into the water, then dove and started

swimming for all I was worth. I could feel Lucas beside me. I reached the other side, clambered out, and touched the tree. Lucas was even with me. So was Moses, barking and jumping.

"Get off," Lucas yelled at him.

I made it into the water first on account of Moses, but I could feel Lucas gaining with every stroke. My skirt wrapped around my legs, and my arms strained with effort. I longed to stop and kick off my clothes, but I couldn't.

I turned my head to grab a breath of air. Moses paddled next to me with a doggy grin on his face, and next to him swam Lucas. I kicked for all I was worth, trying to break free of the skirt that tangled in my legs. I lunged for the shore. I wouldn't let him beat me! I scrambled out just moments before Lucas.

"I win!" I hollered. Moses thought it was a big game. He barked and shook, then splashed back in the river, ready to go again.

Lucas and I stood with our hands on our knees, trying to catch our breath.

"Reckon you *can* swim," Lucas said finally.

"Told you!" I declared. Then I felt bad because it sounded like bragging. "It *was* mighty close." I wondered how he got to be such a good swimmer.

"Why aren't you swimming downstream with all the others?"

"Them?" Lucas shrugged and waved his hand. "Aw, they ain't nothin'." I saw him bite his lip, then he turned away and pulled his boot over his crumpled foot.

"Jo?" He turned back and looked at me with wide eyes. "You ain't gonna tell no one you beat me, are you?"

"No!" I'd never live it down if folks knew I'd been swimming with a colored boy. "You're not gonna tell, are you?"

"No!"

"Okay, then. No one's got to know. 'Specially not your ma."

"'Specially not her."

I walked to where I had my towel and dried my face. Then I grabbed my book.

"What's that?" Lucas asked.

"*The Adventures of Huckleberry Finn,*" I said, showing him the cover. "You ever read it?"

"Naw." He looked away like he didn't care. "What's it about?"

"It's about this boy, Huck Finn, and this slave named Jim who run away on a raft down the Mississippi River. They aim to get Jim to Cairo so's he can go north and be free, but they miss it in the fog. Then they nearly get run over by a steamboat."

"No kidding? Are they killed?"

"Huck ain't, but I don't know about Jim. I was just getting to that part."

"Really?"

There was something about the look in his eyes that made me blurt, "You want to listen?" The minute the words left my mouth, I felt stupid.

He thought about it for a good minute. I could see his mind tugging this way and that. Finally he looked around like he was checking that no one was spying on us, then he nodded. "Okay. Just for a bit, though."

I settled on the fallen log, and Lucas sat on a stump just nearby. I cracked open the book and began reading about the Grangerfords and Shepherdsons and Huck finding Jim again. After two chapters my voice wore out, so I closed the book.

"What happens next?" Lucas asked.

"I don't know. My voice is too tired to read any more."

"Let me have it, then."

I handed him the book, and he started reading. He read smooth and easy, not stumbling over the words like I sometimes did. I leaned back on the log and stared up at the clouds and listened to the river flowing.

Lucas reached the end of the chapter and closed the book. "Wanna see somethin'?" he asked.

I looked at him, feeling suspicious but mighty curious, too. "Okay." I shrugged.

"Come on, then." He stood and led the way into the woods, ducking past underbrush and around trees. He shoved through what looked like an impenetrable wall of brambles. I followed him, surprised to see a path between the thorns. Lucas stopped. I looked around and found myself in a grassy clearing surrounded by prickle bushes.

"Lookit." He pointed to the edge of a clearing. A tiny rabbit huddled under a sort of miniature lean-to. I watched as it let Lucas walk right up to it.

"How'd you do that?" I asked.

Lucas picked up the rabbit. "Get back, Moses," he said. Moses backed away and whined. Lucas showed me the rabbit.

"I found 'im in the woods," he said. "He'd got swiped at by an animal or a trap or somethin' an' had a rip clean across his side." Lucas pointed to a streak of matted fur and what looked like mud. "I been fixin' him up."

I reached out and touched the rabbit's head. His fur was silky soft.

"Simon, that's my brother, Simon says I got a way with hurt things. He says if we're gonna get anywhere, we gotta work harder and be smarter than other folks. So I'm practicin' on these animals."

"Practicing to do what?" The rabbit's eyes were like liquid pools. He trembled, and Lucas let him down.

"To fix things. Simon says there's a whole world of things that need fixin'. I aim to start with these animals." Lucas glanced at me. "I never showed this to no one before, but I figured you're out here so much, when you see any other animals hurt, you could bring 'em to me."

I nodded eagerly. "I will," I said. "Can I help, too?"

He studied me for a minute, then shrugged. "You can't tell no one. It's a secret. Swear."

"I swear."

"And you gotta come back with that book. So I can see how it ends."

I nodded. "Deal."

My stomach rumbled then, and the look of the sky said it was getting late. Time to leave the woods and head for home. My skirt swung stiffly around my knees. I was streaked with red mud and smelled like river water, but I didn't care. For the first time since coming to Jericho, I felt happy.

chapter six

I spent the next two days at the river, reading about Huckleberry and watching that rabbit get better. Lucas found a turtle with a leg tangled up with fishing line, and he fixed that, too. It was the snapping kind of turtle, though, so we didn't get too close. It bit a stick as thick as my finger clean in half. Lucas got all the fishing line out, then let the turtle go. He said he wasn't going to mess with it more than that. I didn't blame him.

Mama was expecting a surprise on Friday morning, so I aimed to stay home and see what it was. She danced around the house without any shoes on, whistling and giggling. It had to be something special.

"What is it, Mama?" I asked her as she peered out the window.

"You'll see."

All I knew was that it was being delivered and that it was a surprise. I crossed my fingers and hoped and hoped it was a television. Daddy hated television, but I thought if Mama got her mind set firm on having one, then maybe.

At midmorning, a white pickup truck pulled alongside the parsonage. Two men got out, then lifted something boxed up and heavy between them. The box read Pierson's Appliance and Hardware on the side. My heart soared. It looked just the right size for a TV.

Mama let the men in the house and showed them where to put the box. Then she signed some papers and handed them back. The men left without saying ten words.

Mama and I stared at the box. The silence grew. Finally I couldn't stand it anymore. "Aren't you going to open it?"

"First thing of luxury I ever bought with my very own money," she said. "I'm just savoring the moment."

I bounced on my toes. I was having a hard time savoring anything. I wanted to see what was in there. Finally Mama got a knife from the kitchen and slit the top and sides of the cardboard. The box fell away. I leaned forward in anticipation, then settled back with a sigh. It wasn't a television.

Mama, though, was grinning from ear to ear. "Look at this," she said. "It's a brand-new Silvertone console with a walnut casing." She ran her hand over the smooth surface. "Isn't it beautiful?"

It was then I noticed that our old radio was gone. I hadn't missed it. It was an old thing from before I was born with a cracked casing and a tuner knob that jiggled loose. It took a kind of magic hand to find a station. If we did get music to play, it crackled and spit so badly that it was next to impossible to make out the song. Whenever we turned it on, I swear the mockingbird outside sang louder and sweeter just for spite.

"Sure is, Mama." I swallowed down my initial disappointment that it wasn't a television. The polished wood shone, and the knobs on the radio gleamed. I touched the tuner and felt firm pressure. The needle on the front moved slowly back and forth.

"Let's put some music on." Mama ran to her bedroom. She returned carrying a box of records that were hers and Daddy's. We hadn't listened to them in months, ever since the old record player started habitually scratching the length of whatever it was playing.

Mama and I flipped through the stack. Tommy Dorsey, Glenn Miller, and Duke Ellington; Mahalia Jackson and Rosemary Clooney. I ran my hand along the cover of a George Gershwin record. Once, when I was eight and we were living in Ohio, I woke to the sound of music and laughter. I peeked into the living room and saw Mama and Daddy dancing to "I Got Rhythm" with the light of the moon streaming through the window. I felt so embarrassed that I hurried back to my room, though I couldn't help but smile as I lay in my bed, listening to the music.

"Let's listen to Perry Como," Mama said, pulling out a record. "We can dance."

She tenderly put the record on the turntable and set the needle down gently. There was a brief pause, then sweet, mellow music pulsed into the air. I took a look outside to see what that old mockingbird thought about it all. The bird sat on the branch of the tree. He cocked his head. I could have sworn he was listening.

Mama grabbed my hands and twirled me around. I laughed as I spun. Mama had taught me all the dances— the waltz, the Charleston, the fox-trot. She learned them from her mama. I hadn't known Grandma very long, she died when I was young, but I sure remembered how she could move her feet whenever a fiddle started playing.

Most good Baptist folks thought fast music and dancing were grievous sins right up there with murder and divorce. If that was the case, then Mama was going straight to the devil. That used to scare the daylights out of me. But Mama said she guessed God liked music, it was just that not everybody knew that about Him.

Mama leaned me into a dip so low, my head nearly touched the floor, then pulled me up and twirled me again. We were laughing and dancing so hard that we didn't hear the front door open.

"What is this?" Daddy slammed the door behind him. Mama and I turned to see Daddy striding into the house toward the phonograph. He moved the needle off the record with a loud screech.

"Maye, what is this?" Daddy asked. He glared at the new radio.

"Isn't it beautiful?" Mama said, walking toward him. I could tell she was trying to pretend she didn't notice that he was mad. "It's my surprise. I told you I was buying a surprise."

"I thought you meant a new dress or a hat!" Daddy said. He looked at Mama, then at Mama's bare feet, then at me. His mouth set in a firm line. I cringed, wondering what I had done wrong.

"Joseph, what is the matter?" Mama asked. She folded her arms across her chest.

Daddy huffed. "I could hear that music clear down the street. What if someone heard you? One of the deacons?"

Mama shrugged and shook her head. "Why would that matter?"

"It's different here," Daddy said. "I've forgotten how different. Several of the deacons were just talking the other day about what awful music is filling the airways and corrupting the minds of our children. What if they had walked by the parsonage on their way to the church and heard what was coming out of this?" He pointed to the new phonograph. I looked at it, wondering if it might suddenly emit something awful.

"Perry Como?" Mama asked.

"They could have thought it was Elvis or one of those others."

"Who cares what they might have thought!" Mama's eyes flashed. "You are so concerned about what *they* think that you are forgetting what *you* think. You love music."

Daddy didn't say anything to that. He just marched into the bedroom, got a tie, and marched out. Mama watched him go. A look of hurt flashed across her face. She walked away from the console without turning it back on. Outside, the mockingbird sang a few trilling notes.

I was in my room after lunch, thinking about getting my things to go to the river. I heard a knock at the front door, then Mama called, "Josephine!"

I hurried out of my room, wondering who it could be. Bobby Sue stood in the middle of the living room. I nearly gasped with surprise. She looked so pretty, with her golden hair pulled back in barrettes and a blue scarf around her neck.

"Hello, Josephine," she said.

"Hello," I managed. I couldn't believe she was here, talking to me, after I'd been so shamed at the five-and-ten.

"Would you like some lemonade, Bobby Sue?" Mama asked, coming to my rescue. "Fresh squeezed this morning."

"Yes, thank you." Bobby Sue smiled, then she looked around the room. Her eyes lit upon the new console, and her face glowed.

"I heard you got a new Silvertone," she said. "Martha Pierson told me. It sure is beautiful."

"Yes, it is. Thank you," Mama said without much enthusiasm. She handed Bobby Sue and me each a glass of lemonade. The cool, sweaty glass tingled against my skin. I took a sip. My throat felt parched.

Bobby Sue waited until Mama went back into the kitchen before she sidled up to me. "I thought we could listen to your Elvis records on your new phonograph," she said in a hushed voice.

My heart stopped, then sped up again, twice as fast. I had forgotten about that, about my lie at the drugstore. It had been almost two weeks ago. I searched my brain for something to say.

"Oh, okay," I said stupidly. "Let's just go into my room for a minute."

"You are so lucky," Bobby Sue said as she followed me to my room. "My daddy hates Elvis. Called him a heathen playing jungle music. Can you believe that?"

I nodded, but I barely heard a word she'd said. *What am I going to do?* I asked myself. *What am I going to do?* I opened a dresser drawer and tried to pretend like I was looking for something.

"I know they're in here somewhere," I mumbled.

Bobby Sue sat on my bed and crossed her legs. "I'm going to buy a portable record player for my room," she said. "That way Daddy won't even know what I'm listening to. There's this store in Greenville that sells them for only forty-seven dollars and ninety-five cents."

"Wow. That much?" I stopped my pretend searching and stared at her. I couldn't imagine having that much money. The most I'd ever had at any one time was nine dollars and eighty-seven cents, and that was when I was saving for a bicycle.

"Yeah, but listen to this. You only have to pay one dollar down and one dollar a week! I'd do it in a minute if we lived in Greenville."

I had a sudden idea. "Let's go to Pierson's and see if they sell them there."

Bobby Sue shook her head. "They don't have them yet. Martha promised to tell me the minute they came in."

I deflated. What was I going to do? "You, uh, want to go to the soda shop?" I asked.

"Let's listen to Elvis first," Bobby Sue said. "I want to hear 'Don't Be Cruel.' Then we can go and brag to everyone."

"Oh, sure." My mouth tasted like I had swallowed a handful of sand. I went back to rummaging through the drawer.

"Haven't you found them yet?" Bobby Sue asked. She leaned over me and peered into the drawer. I quickly closed it.

"I just can't remember where I put them." I walked across the room and opened my closet. "After we moved." I made a show of looking through the closet.

"Well, do you have them or not?"

I tried to swallow. "Maybe they're still in a box somewhere," I said.

Bobby Sue huffed. "Ask your mom, then."

"She wouldn't know," I said quickly. I closed the closet door. "Let's go do something. We could go to Harper's and look at *Silver Screen*. I'll, uh, I'll find them later." I looked at her and tried to smile.

Bobby Sue crossed her arms. "I don't believe you really have any Elvis records," she said.

"I do, I—"

"You're a liar, Josephine Clawson!" Bobby Sue declared. "And I bet your daddy won't let you listen to Elvis, either. You're a liar *and* a Goody Two-shoes, and I'm going to tell everyone the truth about you!"

Bobby Sue marched out of my room. "Good-bye, Mrs. Clawson," she said to my mother, who was sitting on the sofa, darning some of Daddy's socks. "I'm going now."

"Good-bye." Mama watched her as she stormed out of the house. Then she turned to look at me. She raised her eyebrows, questioning.

I shook my head and tried to keep from crying. I couldn't tell Mama what I'd done. She'd be so disappointed. Not on account of Elvis, but on account of me lying.

I waited until I could trust myself to speak, then I sat on the sofa next to her.

"Why can't we go back to Indiana?" I asked finally.

Mama sighed. She rested the sock in her lap. "Our life is here now," she said. "In Jericho."

Daddy's life was here, I thought bitterly. Mine certainly wasn't. And Mama could make a life anywhere. "I don't have any friends here." My voice clutched. Tears pricked dangerously at the back of my eyelids.

Mama wrapped her arm around me and pulled me close. "Oh, Jo," she said. "I'm sorry. It's hard, baby. I know." She paused, then her voice brightened. "But school starts in a week and a half. You'll make plenty of friends once school starts."

School. That's what I was dreading most of all. Surviving the summer without any friends was one thing, but how would I possibly survive school?

chapter seven

"Guess what I found!" Lucas said.

"What?" It was Saturday morning. Mama and Daddy were at a breakfast for the Jericho Missionary Aid Society. I begged out of it, then escaped to the river. I had decided that I would spend every moment possible at the river until school started. There wasn't any reason for me to go into town, except to return my library books. I sure didn't want to see any of the girls from my Sunday school class.

I found Lucas at the clearing, fussing over his rabbit. It was fully healed and ready to be set free. We took it to a rabbit warren Lucas knew about, set it on the ground, and watched. It hopped forward, twitched its nose, and hopped again. Finally it seemed to remember something. It bounded forward and disappeared into the woods. Then Lucas turned to me with bright eyes.

"Guess!"

I shrugged. "Not another turtle?" I asked, frowning. It was a miracle we'd each kept all our fingers after rescuing the last one.

Lucas shook his head. "Nope, better." His eyes were shining.

"What is it, then?" His excitement was catching. I bounced on my toes.

"'Member how you were sayin' you wanted some adventure? After we finished readin' 'bout Huckleberry?"

I nodded. I was plumb tired of being civilized all the time. I wanted to light out for something grand.

"Whad'ya you say 'bout us buildin' a raft an' floatin' down the river?" Lucas's grin nearly split his face.

"What are you talking about?"

"I found some logs," Lucas said. "Not too big, neither. They fell off the sawmill truck with a big old crash. Nobody come back for 'em. They're still there."

"You found some logs?" The possibility of what he was saying started to grow in my mind. "We could build a raft! Our very own raft!"

Lucas nodded. Then his expression darkened.

"Can't tell nobody, though." He looked around like somebody might be spying on us. "Nobody."

"Who'm I gonna tell?" I wondered aloud. "Come on, let's get started!"

Lucas and I stared into the ditch. There were seven logs down there, just off the side of the road. Each was about the size of Lucas, smooth and fresh cut, smelling of pine.

"How we gonna get 'em out?" Lucas asked.

"It can't be too hard." I scrambled into the ditch, grabbed the top log, and heaved. It didn't budge. I took a better grip and heaved again. The log creaked but didn't move an inch.

Lucas peered down at me. "That ain't gonna work. You won't be able to carry 'em out. Not with me helpin', neither."

"Who made you such an expert, Lucas Jefferson?" Sweat dripped down my forehead. I was hot and cranky. "You got a better idea?"

Lucas thought for what seemed like a good long minute. "Let's get us some vines," he said finally. "And make a kind of pulley. I seen Simon do something like it when he was workin' on Uncle Obadiah's roof."

We collected some vines, strong and supple ones, then Lucas showed me how to set it up. We looped the vines over a tree branch, then tied one end to the log. We held on to the other end. The vines shuddered, but we heaved those logs out of the ditch and set to rolling them to the river. It was dirty work on account of all the trees and brush in the way. We looked a bit like a pair of mules, but we got all seven of those logs out of the ditch and down to the edge of the river.

"We did it!" I raised my arms in victory, then collapsed on the stack of logs. Sweat dripped off my forehead and stung my eyes. I wiped them with my shirt, then rooted around for the thermos of lemonade I'd brought with me. I took a long swig, then handed it to Lucas. He was drenched in sweat and streaked with red mud. He looked near collapse. He took a drink and handed it back. We passed this way, back and forth, until the lemonade was gone.

"I got to get home, before Mama and Daddy catch me looking like this," I said. I grimaced at the sight of my muddy clothes. "Be out here tomorrow." I caught myself. Tomorrow was church. "No, Monday. We'll get the raft finished next week, before school starts."

Lucas nodded. He looked over the logs. "Monday. Soon's I'm done with chores an' such."

I walked home. Every muscle in my body ached. It was the good kind of ache, though. It wasn't until I was home and washed that I realized what I'd done. I'd drunk out of the same thermos as Lucas Jefferson. But nothing bad had happened. Fire hadn't rained down from heaven, my skin hadn't broken out in hives, and no one had been around to laugh and point. When it was just me and Lucas, things seemed regular, almost like our different colors didn't matter. I rolled that thought over in my mind, then held it close for safe-keeping. Thoughts like that get muddled when said out loud.

Lucas and I spent a solid week making that raft. It was harder work than we'd thought, getting those logs tied together even and straight with no chinks or holes. We blistered our hands trying to tighten the ropes. I thought Huckleberry'd had it easy. He *found* his raft.

School started on a Tuesday, the day after Labor Day. I had wanted to take the raft out the Saturday before, but it wasn't ready yet. We decided to wait and go on Monday. Mama and Daddy were driving to Greenville for a pastors' picnic. Abilene was going to spend part of the morning at the parsonage, but then she had to go to a quilting party for a neighbor who was expecting. I'd be spending the day having a grand adventure.

Monday morning dawned clear and bright. Outside my window, the mockingbird mimicked a cardinal's song. I bounded out of bed, then got myself ready for a day on the water.

"What you up to, Miss Jo?" Abilene asked. She eyed me as I snuck about the house, gathering supplies.

"Nothing." I froze, a fishing pole hidden behind my back.

"Sure got a lot goin' on fer nothin'," she said.

I shrugged and tried a smile on her. She shook her head, then went back to work in the kitchen. I finished stowing my things in a towel.

"Don't be doing nothin' to get yourself in trouble."

I jumped. I hadn't realized she was still watching me. I wondered how much she knew.

"No'm," I said.

"And take some of my sweet tea case you get thirsty doin' nothin'." She handed me a thermos.

"Thank you!" I sidled out the back door. "Bye, now."

She watched me go, still wagging her head.

I skipped behind the Farm and Fleet toward the woods, feeling free. The air was hot and steamy. It had rained hard and steady yesterday. Puddles of red mud dotted my path. Daddy was upset it had rained because it kept folks out of church. That meant less money for the offering plate. I was glad because the river would be up and flowing strong.

Lucas and Moses were waiting when I got to the river. Lucas stood and brushed off his overalls. "Ready?" he asked.

I nodded. A lump of excitement welled in my chest. "Ready." I stowed my towel filled with provisions in the middle of the raft. It was a good-looking raft, I thought. Just the right size for Lucas and me and even Moses, if he sat down and didn't move too much.

"Let's go, then." Lucas licked his lips. I guess he was excited, too.

Lucas put Moses on the raft first, with a firm warning to lay down and not move. Lucas and I grabbed hold of the raft, then pushed it into the shallows of the river. We waited until it was floating and even, then climbed on. It wobbled, but Lucas and I steadied it with poles that we'd fashioned from branches. Soon we were in the middle of the river, floating away on the current.

"We're moving!" I hollered. Lucas gave a whoop. Moses barked.

Lucas and I looked at Moses in fear. "Sit, Moses," he commanded. Moses was our biggest concern. If he got to barking and jumping, he could tip us right over. Moses sat. Lucas and I grinned, then floated in silence. The raft seemed to want to spin, so Lucas and I had to pole to keep it straight.

We floated past the colored swimming hole, both sighing with relief that it was deserted this early in the day. I had been ready to jump overboard and swim underwater if we'd seen any people there. That was our last obstacle. Now we were home free.

"Reckon I'll be Huckleberry Finn and you can be Ole Jim," I said when we were sufficiently under way.

Lucas whirled around to look at me, causing the raft to wobble. "I won't!"

I looked at him in alarm. "Why not?"

"I aim to be Huckleberry."

"You can't be Huckleberry," I said, trying to talk reason. "You ain't white. You're colored, so you have to be Ole Jim."

"Well, you ain't a boy, and Huckleberry's a boy. So there." That remark stung.

"You shut up, Lucas! I say you gotta be Ole Jim."

"Well, I say I ain't! Simon says colored folks can be most anythin' they want."

"Can't be white," I muttered. I glared at Lucas, and he glared right back. I swear Lucas was the most stubborn person I'd ever laid eyes on. "You gotta be Jim!"

"I don't!"

"Do so!"

"Don't!"

I stood and lunged toward Lucas, meaning to scare him. He drew back, thrusting his pole forward. I tripped and caught my foot on the end of it. The pole went flying, landing with a splash. Moses barked, then leapt into the water after it. I lost my balance. I waved my arms wildly, then fell off the raft. The river was deep here, over my head, and the current clutched at my legs. I treaded water, trying to get my bearings, then flung my arm over the raft and fought to hang on. The raft began to spin. Lucas reached for my hand but stumbled. The raft wobbled and bucked. I was pulling myself back onto the raft when Moses swam up with Lucas's pole in his mouth. He surged toward the raft and planted his two front feet on top as he clawed his way up.

"He's going to break it up!" I yelled. Water splashed into my face.

Moses clawed at one of the ropes tying the logs together. "Get your dog!" I screamed.

"Moses, no!" Lucas grabbed for Moses, but the weight of all of us on one side caused the raft to tilt. Lucas lost his balance, waved his arms, and jumped over me into the river. The raft stood crazily on end, then tilted toward me, blocking out the sun.

chapter eight

"Jo! Hey, Jo!

"Jo! Come on, Jo!" Someone slapped me over and over on both cheeks.

I opened my eyes. Lucas Jefferson's face swam into view. "Stop that! Stop hitting me."

He sighed then and leaned back. "Whew," he said. "I thought you was a goner."

Moses nosed in and began licking my face. I squirmed to get away. "Stop it!" I struggled to push Moses away from me and sit up. When I did, a low, throbbing pain started just behind my eyeballs.

"Oh," I groaned, holding my head. "My head hurts."

"You got a goose egg the size of a baseball," Lucas said.

I reached up to touch it, wincing.

"That raft done a number on you. You went under like a rock. I thought you was gonna drown." Lucas's eyes were wide, his face pinched.

I remembered the raft coming toward me but nothing after that. Without warning, tears flooded my eyes. I puckered my face to try and hold them back, but it didn't do any good. They spilled down my cheeks. I angrily tried to wipe them away, but they came too fast. Lucas must have thought me a baby, but there wasn't anything I could do about it. I sat there sobbing and feeling foolish for a good, long time.

Lucas didn't say a thing, didn't even laugh.

Finally I was able to take some ragged breaths and wipe my eyes. "Where's the raft?"

Lucas shrugged and stared at the river. He shook his head. "It just kept spinnin' down the river. Prob'ly still goin'. Good riddance is what I say."

I moaned. "After all that work." I held my head in my hands. "What about our food and towels and everything?"

"All gone. Everythin's gone. The current's powerful strong 'cause of that rain."

I couldn't think straight to know what had happened. All I knew was that I had an awful headache, our raft was lost, and we didn't have any food or fishing poles or towels or anything. I wondered how I'd managed to swim to shore with my head hurting the way it did.

"This is all your fault. If you'd only been Ole Jim . . . ," I growled, holding my head and rising to my feet.

Dizziness hit me. I sat down, feeling slightly green.

"What is it?" Lucas asked. "What's wrong?"

"I don't feel so good." I tried to keep the tears out of my voice. I thought I might throw up.

Lucas stared at me. "You're pale as a ghost," he said. "Here, bend down and put your head between your feet." He pushed on my back, forcing my head down.

"What are you doing?" I asked, but I complied. The world didn't spin quite so much down here.

"You may have a concussion," Lucas said.

"What do you know about it?" I was wet and dirty and in pain. All I wanted to do was get home, curl up on my bed, and take a long nap. I didn't want to talk to Lucas Jefferson about my having a concussion, whatever that was.

"You feel like you're gonna throw up?" Lucas asked.

I watched an ant struggle over a twig on the forest floor. "Not now. It's better now."

I heard Lucas stand and walk around me. I was still

studying the ant. My head didn't hurt as much that way.

"We got to get ice on your head," he said. "And you should probably see a doctor."

"Maybe someone will come along."

"Only folks come 'round here are bootleggers and hunters. It ain't huntin' season."

I felt Lucas touch my head, the area right around where I'd been hit. He parted my hair with his fingers and stared at my scalp. "What are you doing?" I held myself still and stiff.

"Lookin' to see if you fractured your skull."

That sounded scary. My heart pounded in my chest. "Have I?"

"Don't think so. Seems just a regular knock on the head."

"I'm not a rabbit or a turtle or one of your sick animals," I said, feeling grumpy. "I'm a person."

Lucas shrugged. "Simon says lots of times folks ain't so different from animals. 'Cept sometimes animals are kinder."

"Simon says, Simon says," I muttered under my breath. I was starting not to like Simon very much, and I'd never even met him.

A jab of pain hit me between the eyes.

"What are we gonna do?" We hadn't talked too much about how we were going to get home, after our grand adventure. Some adventure it turned out to be. We were lost, out here in the middle of nowhere.

"Stand up," Lucas said.

He pulled me to my feet. I closed my eyes as the world began doing a slow-motion spin. "I'm still dizzy and my head is throbbing." My voice came out sounding like a whine. I wanted to bite my tongue.

Lucas looked at the river, then surveyed the woods.

"We're quite a ways from home, but we ain't too far—"

"'Cause you were being obstinate," I muttered.

"Still a pretty fair piece from your house."

"If you'd have just listened to me in the first place—"

"My house is just a few miles through them woods. Reckon we could go there, first."

I stopped muttering and stared at him.

"You're going to take me to the Quarters?"

Lucas snorted. "You scared?"

"No," I lied. I didn't want to be scared, but something about me couldn't help it. I looked at him steadily to prove my courage, but my heart was tripping double time. As much as I was curious to see the Quarters, I'd always imagined going in with an adult. An adult like Mama. It didn't seem such a good idea to go by myself.

Lucas crossed his arms over his chest and stared at me with disdain.

"I ain't scared! Just, Mama and Daddy will be starting to wonder where I am."

"We were gonna be on the river all day!" Lucas reminded me. "You weren't gonna be home anyway."

"I'm just saying . . ." I closed my eyes and rubbed my forehead. "Let's go, then."

I'd have never made it if not for Lucas. I didn't know where we were or where we were going. I suppose I could have followed the river, but my brain was so muddled that I'd have probably ended up walking in circles. I felt weak and close to throwing up. After just a few hundred yards Lucas offered to let me put my arm around his shoulders. I did, and that steadied me some. We walked for what seemed like hours. I wanted to stop and take a nap, but Lucas wouldn't let me. He made me keep walking.

Lucas was the closest thing I had to a friend in all of Jericho. The thought hit me like a jolt. I was glad no one could read my mind. If folks knew I'd even thought such a thing, they'd probably treat me like Lenore Cooper, or worse, since I ought to know better. I'd be scorned right out of Jericho. White trash, that's what they'd call me.

I snuck a glance at Lucas out of the corner of my eye. He had a look of concentration on his face as he trudged forward. He was the gentlest, laughingest, most contrary person I'd ever met.

I figured I was just thinking crazy, all befuddled in my brain. Lucas and me, we weren't friends. We could never be friends. I'd just had a knock on the head, that's what.

Maybe it was because I wasn't feeling well, but a shot of sadness ripped through me. I had to firmly clench my jaw to keep from crying again.

chapter nine

The Quarters was a neighborhood of ramshackle timber frame houses huddled at the edge of the scrubby wood. The houses all looked old and tired, like they'd seen a life of heavy work and needed to sit down and rest.

Lucas helped me up the cracked steps and through the front door of his house. He sat me down on a battered old sofa. It had been patched in several places with faded calico and stained denim. A red-and-blue afghan was thrown over the back.

"Mama!" Lucas called.

I glanced around. The house was a tiny clapboard that looked like it might fall down if the wind blew too hard. There wasn't a dining room, just the living room, a kitchen, and two tiny bedrooms that I could see from my vantage point on the sofa. A shotgun house, that's what Mama called 'em. You could shoot a gun through the front door and it'd pass clean out the back, it was that small. One of the windows was cracked, but it was dressed up nice with the same faded calico as the couch. The house smelled good, like corn bread and mint tea.

"Mama!" Lucas called again. No one answered. He marched into the kitchen.

"LouEllen," I heard him say. "Where's Mama?"

"She went to the quiltin' party after work," said the voice of a little girl. "Look at you, Lucas! What happened? You get caught in a mud storm or something? Mama's gonna tan you silly for messin' your clothes."

"Don't you worry 'bout it. What you doin'?"

"Gettin' dinner ready. Simon's still gone. Maybe he got a job today. I heard the Jenkins folks was lookin' for pickers."

"Jenkins is scrub farmers," Lucas said. "An' you don't know nothin' 'bout cookin' dinner."

"Do so! What you doin' with that ice, Lucas?"

"None of your business."

"But Mama just got that from Tanner Adams. She was gonna use it for lemonade, it being the first day of school tomorrow."

"I ain't gonna take it all. 'Sides, it's gonna melt soon anyway."

I listened to the two argue. I knew Abilene had three children, but the only one I'd ever met was Lucas. I looked around the little room, trying to get a glimpse of what it was like to live here.

Lucas walked back in the room with a towel, a basin of water, and a chunk of ice wrapped in a dishrag. "You need to be gettin' cleaned up. Then put this ice on your head. Mama's not here, but Simon'll be back soon. He'll know how to get you home."

I took the ice, feeling foolish. "Can I use your bathroom? Maybe I could rinse off a bit."

Lucas jerked his thumb over his shoulder. "Out back."

"Oh!" An outhouse. I felt my face turn crimson. "Uh . . . I'll be okay."

I dipped the towel in the basin and wiped my face. The water felt cool against my skin. Some of my dizziness ebbed. I rinsed my arms and tried to clean off as much of the mud and grime as I could with Lucas standing right there watching. Then I gingerly put the ice on top of my head. I gasped as the cold touched my bruise.

LouEllen scampered into the living room. Her eyes grew wide as she looked me over. I studied her right back. She was tiny and quick, her hair done up in pig-tails and pink bows that jiggled when she moved. I smiled at her. "Hey," I said. "My name's Jo."

She grinned, showing a gap where her two front teeth were missing. She quickly covered her mouth with her hands, then looked at Lucas.

"What she doin' here, Lucas?" she whispered, not taking her eyes off of me.

"I got hurt," I said, trying to find the words to explain what had happened. I leaned my head over. "See?"

Her mouth formed a little red *O*. "She gonna be okay?" LouEllen asked, still staring at me but talking to Lucas.

"Yeah. Don't be so nosy."

"It's okay," I said. "I don't mind."

The front door banged open. We all jumped and turned toward the sound. A grown Negro walked in. He was lugging a television, so he didn't see me at first, but when he did, he nearly dropped it. He set the television on an overturned crate next to the sofa, then stared at me.

"Hello," I said in a tiny voice. My mouth felt dry. This had to be Simon.

Simon stared at Lucas and LouEllen, fire shooting out of his eyes.

"What's going on?" he asked. "Is Ma here?"

"She's at the quiltin' bee," LouEllen said. She peered around him. "You got a television!"

"It ain't ours. I borrowed it." He jerked his hand toward me. "What is she doin' here?" he asked in a loud whisper.

"Lucas brung her." LouEllen peeked at me from behind her older brother. I smiled nervously and licked my lips.

"Lucas!" Simon's voice was angry. He turned to look at me, then he grabbed Lucas by the arm and dragged him into the kitchen. LouEllen followed, taking quick glances back at me.

"What you doin' bringin' a white girl into our house, specially when you know Ma ain't home?" Simon's voice was angry and low. I chewed on the edge of my thumb.

"It's Jo Clawson," Lucas said. "The preacher's girl from Mama's work."

"Why's she here?"

"She got hurt. I thought maybe . . ."

"Lucas!" Simon hollered. Then his voice lowered to a fierce whisper. "You lost your senses? Folks start missing her an' the sheriff turns up here lookin'? Gonna get us all killed!"

"They wouldn't look here," Lucas said. He didn't

sound convinced. His voice trembled. "Whadja want me to do with her?"

"Not bring her here! Why's she all muddy?"

"She fell in the river."

"Don't tell me no more. Don't say nothing else. You want to ruin everything we're tryin' to do?"

"No!" It sounded like Lucas had angry tears in his voice. I gnawed my thumb, and my eyes darted around the room, looking for an escape. "How we gonna get her home?"

"I don't know, Lucas! I got a bunch of folks coming over for a meeting. Be here any minute now. She's gotta be gone!"

I bit the edge of my thumb so hard, I tasted blood. A chill washed over me, sending goose prickles across my arm. The anger in Simon's voice was heavy enough to taste. I stood quickly. The world turned instantly black. I clutched the edge of the sofa, then took unsteady steps toward the door.

"Jo. Where you goin'?" Lucas was instantly beside me.

"Home. I'm going home."

I opened the front door with a loud squeak and stepped onto the sagging porch. I tried hard to keep my eyes forward, to not look at Lucas. I could still feel Simon's anger in the room.

"You can't go by youself. What if you fall?"

"I'm fine!" I turned and glared at Lucas. "Just leave me alone. You've caused enough trouble for one day."

"Me? You're the one who—"

"Lucas!" Simon's voice rang across the house.

"Let me at least walk you to the fence. Just to see you get safe to your road. It ain't far from there."

"I can do it! I'm fine!" I shoved past him and started down the stairs. Then the stairs blurred out of focus. My legs went weak.

"Darned fool girl," Lucas muttered. He grabbed my arms and steadied me. "Stubborn as an old donkey." Lucas walked me down the steps. "Jest wait right there an' I'll get you home."

❧

Lucas pulled me down the road in an old wagon layered with burlap bags. It smelled like potatoes. The dust from the bags itched my nose. The wagon made a creak-thump, creak-thump as it jostled over the ruts and bumps. I hung on to the sides to keep my balance. I was too tired to care how stupid I must look.

The sun was just a sliver on the horizon when we reached the fence. The world was dusky, and shadows moved in unexpected places. Crickets sang, and far off I heard the croak of swamp frogs. I thought about rattlesnakes and coyotes and was glad Lucas was along.

Lucas paused at the fork, glanced around, then turned on Plantation Drive. I was almost home.

A car came from the other direction and caught us in the glare of its headlights. The hair on Moses's back bristled. He let out a low growl. Lucas jerked his head away, shielded his eyes, and whispered, "Don't say nothin'."

I covered my eyes with my hand until the car pulled alongside us. A window rolled down. Bobby Sue Snyder stuck her head out. I felt my heart sink into my stomach and thought I might as well have drowned in the river.

"Josephine Clawson?" She looked me up and down.

"What is going on?" Mr. Snyder, one of the deacons at First Baptist Church, leaned across Bobby Sue to get a better look.

"I got hurt," I said, more to the ground than to them. My face was hot with embarrassment.

Mr. Snyder looked sharply at Lucas, as if seeing him for the first time. "What are you doing, boy?"

"Takin' her home, suh," he said. He looked at the wheels of the car. His voice sounded funny, not like it usually did when he was arguing with me.

"I was just walkin' along an' I saw her an' she said, 'Hey, boy, come here with dat wagon an' take me home.' So I said I would, suh."

I glanced sharply at Lucas. I had said nothing of the kind.

"Is that true?" Mr. Snyder asked me. I felt Lucas stiffen. Moses stood wooden legged and tight.

I nodded. "Uh, yes, sir," I lied. I didn't want Mr. Snyder and Bobby Sue to know what had really happened. I thought it better to risk another lie.

"We'll take you home, Josephine." Mr. Snyder climbed out of his car, walked to the wagon, and pulled me up by lifting under my armpits. Moses bared his teeth, protecting Lucas. Mr. Snyder settled me in the backseat.

"Get along, now," Mr. Snyder said to Lucas.

"Yes, suh," Lucas said.

I felt my cheeks flame. Mr. Snyder put the car in gear, then drove toward the parsonage. I didn't dare risk a glance backward to see what had happened to Lucas.

"Good thing I happened along," Mr. Snyder said. "Bobby Sue and I were just on our way home from Greenville for the Labor Day parade. What happened to you? You look terrible."

My mind went blank. "Uh, I was just out taking a

walk. I, uh—got hit on the head. By a truck. A mill truck. I mean, a rock flew off a truck. And hit me."

I figured God might smite me dead for all the lying I'd been doing, but that was the chance I had to take.

"Oh, my." Mr. Snyder glanced my way. "Josephine, that could be serious. You better have your mama call Dr. Jansen as soon as I get you home."

"Yes, sir. I will."

"You sure are a mess," Bobby Sue said. She turned around and wrinkled her nose.

"Yeah." I closed my eyes and hung my head. "I sure am."

Mr. Snyder pulled into the parsonage's driveway. I rushed to get out of the car. "Thank you, Mr. Snyder, sir. That was right kind of you to pick me up. Good-bye, then."

I tried to hurry in, but Mr. Snyder insisted on helping me up the parsonage's steps and in the front door. I could feel Bobby Sue's stare from the car. I'd never live this down. Never, never, never.

"Jo!" Daddy exploded off the couch when we entered the front door. "Where have you been? We've been worried sick! What happened? What's wrong?"

I was too exhausted to even speak. My head was pounding. Mama wrapped her arms around me and eased me to the couch.

"I found her on the road being pulled in a wagon by a colored boy," Mr. Snyder said with a smile on his face. He looked like he found the whole thing quite amusing. "Seems she got hit in the head or some such, and she enlisted his help to get her home."

"You found her . . . ?" Daddy choked on the words. His face paled. He turned to me. "Jo, are you okay?"

I nodded.

"Where does it hurt?" Mama asked. I pointed to my head. I couldn't very well show her my heart that was breaking with humiliation.

"We're much obliged to you," Daddy said to Mr. Snyder. "Would you care for some coffee? Lemonade, perhaps?"

"No, no, thank you. I must be getting home." Mr. Snyder looked at me and shook his head. "You mind yourself now."

I pretended I hadn't heard him. Once he'd finally gone, Mama went to call the doctor, and Daddy collapsed next to me on the couch. His face looked scrunched.

"Jo, what happened? How did you get hurt? Why are you so dirty?" His words were slow and measured. "What were you doing with a colored boy?"

"Daddy, I . . ." The day, everything that had happened, swirled and spun in my head. My thoughts were muddled and achy, like I was just waking up after a night of bad dreams, and I couldn't remember if I was awake or still dreaming. Tears choked in my throat. I clenched my teeth, but that just made it worse.

"Daddy . . ." My voice cracked. I couldn't form the words I wanted to say. Then Mama was there with her hands on my hair and pulling me close. I buried myself in the crook of her shoulder and let the tears flood out of me. Mama held me tight and let me cry. All the sadness and anger and fear bubbled and frothed and spilled over. I knew things would never be the same again.

chapter ten

Mama didn't let me go to school on account of my concussion. Dr. Jansen had told her to wake me every two hours during the night so I wouldn't slip into a coma. Just about the time I'd start to fall asleep, she was there making me wake up. By morning I was so tired, it was like I hadn't slept at all. Mama let me stay home so I could get my rest. I was going to miss the first day of school, but I didn't mind.

Mama stayed home from work. She didn't get a chance to let Abilene know she didn't need to come, so Miz Abilene showed up right on time. I dreaded seeing her, fearful of what she might say about my being at her house. She didn't say anything, though, just took one look at me and shook her head. She set a teapot to brewing.

"Yarrow tea, that's what you need," Abilene said. She poured hot water into a bowl filled with yellow flowers, then strained it into a cup. She handed it to me. "Jus' the thing for that bruise."

I looked at Mama. She shrugged and gave a little nod, so I guessed it was okay. The nettle tea hadn't worked on my hair, but it hadn't hurt me, either. I took a sip.

The tea was warm and soothing. I finished it, then settled into the sofa. Abilene didn't say another word about me or my bruise or how I'd gotten it. She just bustled around the house, chatting with Mama in that easy way she had.

I spent the day listening to the radio and playing games like checkers and Parcheesi. Mama never let me win on purpose, so when I won checkers twice in a row, I knew it was for real. I wished I could spend all my days like this, home with Mama and never having to go to school. But by dinnertime Mama declared me fit as a fiddle.

"Abilene's tea must have done the trick," she said.

I frowned and wished I'd never drunk it.

That night, the radio news reported on how Arkansas governor Orval Faubus had called the Arkansas National Guard to surround Little Rock Central High School. A look passed between Mama and Daddy, then Daddy got up and clicked off the radio before I could hear why the governor would do such a thing. I wished someone would call the National Guard to surround my school. I thought soldiers with guns and uniforms might be easier to face than a classroom full of sixth-grade girls.

In the morning, Daddy agreed to drive me to school. Normally I would walk, but Mama was afraid I might get dizzy again. So I climbed into our blue Chevy and tried to prepare myself for the day ahead.

Daddy drove down Plantation Drive. He slowed the car at the fork by the Keonee County Farm and Fleet. I glanced to my left and caught a glimpse of the tall fence through the trees.

"Why is that fence there, Daddy?" I ventured to ask as we drove past it before turning onto the right-hand road toward town.

Daddy sighed, then tapped his fingers against the steering wheel. His face furrowed.

"Been there a long time," he said finally.

"Since you were little?" I wondered if Daddy had ever climbed that fence, ever snuck into those woods.

Daddy looked straight ahead, but he seemed to be seeing something other than the main street of town that was approaching. "Didn't look the way it does now, but yes, it was there when I was a boy."

"Will it always be there, then?"

Daddy didn't answer. His eyebrows pulled together, making deep wrinkles on his forehead. We rode in silence until we reached my school. I opened the door and started to climb out.

"It'll take a lot to bring that fence down," Daddy mumbled, almost more to himself than to me. "It'll take blood and tears."

I looked at Daddy curiously. I opened my mouth to ask the questions that swirled in my head, but the bell rang, calling me into school. Daddy waved and pulled away. I slung my books over my shoulder and followed the other students into the building.

When I walked into my classroom, everyone stopped and stared. I took a deep breath and told myself it didn't matter. Bobby Sue caught my eye. I tried to smile and look friendly. She gave a little smirk, then went back to chatting with her friends.

At eight o'clock a second bell rang. The teacher marched into the room and rapped on the desk with a ruler. I sank into my chair with a sigh of relief.

The teacher, Mrs. Millhouse, smiled at me. "You must be Josephine," she said. "Welcome. I do hope you are feeling better?"

"Yes'm," I said. A few kids snickered, but Mrs. Millhouse silenced them with a glare. She was a friendly-looking sort, with short white hair and a face creased with laugh lines. I thought we'd get along just fine.

The morning clipped along. I started to relax, started to think school might not be so bad after all. After lunch we were allowed to go outside for thirty minutes. I was walking across the playground toward the sandlot where the boys played stickball when I heard my name.

A group of girls had surrounded Bobby Sue. She was animatedly telling a story. From the way she glanced over, I knew it was about me. The girls around her barraged her with questions, just loud enough so I could overhear.

"She was in a wagon? With a Negro boy?"

"Was she carrying a Bible? I heard she takes one everywhere," said a girl I had never seen before. I guessed she was a Methodist. I hadn't met those girls yet.

"Why's her face all brown and blotchy?" another girl asked.

I touched my nose. It was red and peeling from hours spent on the river.

"Prob'ly rubbed off that Negro boy."

The girls laughed. My face grew hot with embarrassment.

"Does she really quote Scripture all the time?" asked the Methodist girl.

"She's memorized about a million Bible verses," said Bobby Sue. "She's such a show-off in church." She looked toward me. The other girls giggled. I turned away.

I was not a show-off! I couldn't help being a preacher's kid. I couldn't help that Miss Hasty drilled me with Bible questions. Bobby Sue could memorize just as many verses if she wanted to.

"I can't wait until your party on Saturday," one of the girls said, another one I didn't know. Then they all started talking at once. I squinched my eyes and scowled, trying to feel mad instead of sad. Bobby Sue was having a party, and everyone was invited except me. It wasn't fair! I swiped at my eyes with the back of my hand.

❧

Mama was barefoot in the kitchen plucking a chicken when I got home from school. I wrinkled my nose. It was a bloody, messy business, and I hoped she was almost done so I wouldn't have to help. Mama always bought her chickens fresh from some farmer or other. She said she was born and bred a farmer's daughter and couldn't abide the thought of eating a chicken from Winn-Dixie.

"How was school, Jo?" Mama asked.

"Fine."

Mama washed her hands and dried them, then turned to give me a look. "Sounds like a mighty puny kind of fine." She picked up the chicken and rinsed it under cold water. I tried not to look. I wouldn't be able to eat it later if I imagined it all naked and scrawny like that. "What did you do?"

I shrugged. "Nothing, really. Reading and science and stuff. They're slower in math than my old school, so I already know it all. It's stupid." I kicked at the floor with the toe of my saddle shoe.

Mama turned to look at me. Her hair was falling in steamy curls around her face, and her eyes looked tired. "Josephine! I don't want to hear talk like that."

I scowled. Mama was always telling me I should be grateful for school. She had to quit school in eleventh grade when her daddy died. It was something that rankled in her like a splinter that's stuck in deep, and she took it out on me.

"You try your best in school, you hear me? You get all the learning you can."

I sighed, knowing I'd never win this argument. "Okay, Mama."

"You're smart, baby girl. Someday you'll go to college."

I glanced at Mama in surprise. "College? Daddy says college is too expensive and that there's no use in girls going since they just get married anyway. . . ."

"Don't you worry about that." Mama set her mouth in a determined line. "You just study hard. I'll make sure there's money to get you there. You can study to be a nurse or a teacher or a lawyer or anything."

I wrinkled my nose. I wondered if Mama would have been different if her daddy hadn't died and she had stayed in school. I wondered if she would have gone to college. What if she had? My eyes opened wide at the thought. She might never have married Daddy. I wondered if she ever thought about that.

Mama smiled as if reading my mind. "I love your daddy and I love you," she said. "But I want you to have a choice. Now, go do your homework."

"It's different here, Mama," I said softly, not wanting to leave the warm kitchen.

A look of pain flashed across her face. "It's hard. I know. But you'll adjust, Jo. You always do."

That didn't make me feel any better. I didn't know if I would adjust.

I decided then and there that being alone and friendless was something that sounded romantic in books, but in real life it wasn't that great at all.

chapter eleven

There were nine girls in my sixth-grade class, including me. Seven of them were invited to Bobby Sue's party. That's all they talked about at school the rest of the week. I tried to pretend like I didn't care, but I did. I cared a lot.

I hadn't seen Lucas in four days. Ever since my concussion on Monday, Daddy had stuck close to the house, keeping an eye on me. I was beginning to worry I'd never get to the river again. I'd be forced to spend all of my time alone in my room, doing homework.

Just after breakfast on Saturday morning, the day of Bobby Sue's party, Mama shooed me outside, saying I needed to get some fresh air. I knew it was because she wanted to have some sit-down talk time with Daddy. They were going to argue about something. I could tell by the way my stomach got tight when they looked at each other.

I walked to the log bridge. A grin crept across my face when I saw Lucas was already there, a fishing pole dangling in the water. Moses stretched, then ambled over to give me a sniff.

"You," Lucas said when he saw me. He darted his eyes around, as if there might be someone lurking in the woods. "Looking for another adventure?"

I shrugged. My hand touched the bump on my head. "Catch anything?" I asked.

He pulled up a trotline with a mess of fish. "Got dinner for tonight and maybe tomorrow, too."

I nodded. "Those are some good-looking fish." I sat next to him on the log. Neither of us said anything. The sun danced sparkles on the water, and a school of minnows swam in the shallows. A part of me had a million questions I wanted to ask him about his school and what it was like and if he liked it. But another part of me was embarrassed to be sitting there with him. Because Lucas had walked me through the woods, because Bobby Sue Snyder had seen us together, and because I had been to Lucas's house and knew how poor he was. Church folks always said it was no shame to be poor, but it sure seemed like it the way they were always comparing clothes and cars and how much went into the offering plate.

Finally I worked myself into speaking. "I never did thank you for helping me the other day. Taking me home and all. So thanks."

He shrugged. "'S'okay."

We stared into the water for a minute. My leg twitched, then I jumped to my feet. "Race you," I said. "To the clearing and back." I took a ready stance.

Lucas looked at me, then looked through the woods toward the clearing. He shook his head. "Naw."

I sat back down with a smirk. "'Cause you know you can't beat me."

"Can so!" Lucas's eyes flashed.

I shrugged. "Whatever you say."

Lucas stood. "To the clearing and back. On your mark, get set, GO!"

Lucas took the early lead, but I was right behind him. Twigs cracked under our feet as we raced through the woods. Moses ran beside us, his tongue lolling out of the side of his mouth. Lucas slowed to swerve around the tree, and I surged ahead. I had a moment's indecision when I reached the clearing whether we were to actually go inside it or just turn around. I elected to turn around. Lucas knew the quickest way through the brambles, and I didn't want him getting an advantage. I spun on my foot and raced back toward the log. I passed Lucas as he was coming toward the clearing. Then I heard him turn and chase after me. I was going to win! I pumped my arms and felt the burn in my legs.

My toe hit a tree stump. I stumbled forward, losing my stride. Moses barked. Lucas passed me without slowing. I scrambled forward and raced after him. I couldn't let him beat me! I was close enough behind to reach out and touch his shirt, but I couldn't catch him, couldn't make my legs go any faster.

"I won!" Lucas hollered the moment he reached the log. He raised his arms in the air and jumped around. "I won!"

I leaned over and put my hands on my knees. He beat me. A boy with only half a foot, and he beat me. "Close one," I said. I tried to catch my breath, to pretend I wasn't really winded, that I hadn't really tried my hardest.

Lucas hooted and hollered. I rolled my eyes. He acted like he'd never won a race before.

While Lucas carried on, I sat on the log and looked around. I picked up a book that was lying on the log near his fishing pole. "What is this?" I asked. I turned it over in my hands. It was the grubbiest book I'd ever seen. Half the cover had been ripped off and patched together with cardboard and brown tape. The pages were stained and dog-eared and falling out of the binding. "What happened to your book?"

Lucas stopped bouncing. He looked down at the book and scowled. "Nothin' happened. That's how I got it."

I laughed in disbelief. "Who'd give you a book that looked like that?"

"Got it at school."

I looked at the book in amazement and wondered what kind of school it was to give him a battered book. All the books I'd been given for the year were clean and crisp, with sweet-smelling white pages.

"It looks like it's a million years old," I said.

Lucas snatched the book out of my hands. "Is, practically. Simon says colored schools don't have no money. Can't afford new books. Got to give us the old ones."

"They can't afford books?" Lucas's school sounded as poor as the folks who lived in the Quarters.

"Simon says there ain't such a thing as separate but equal. Never was an' never will be." Lucas clenched his jaw. I could see the muscles hopping up and down. His eyes narrowed.

I didn't know what to say. I sure didn't want to talk

about books anymore. "Let's go hunt the woods, see if there are any hurt animals," I said finally.

Lucas's eyes darted this way and that. He looked like a rabbit, checking for danger. "Naw," he said.

"Why not?"

"Just don't want to."

"Come on. It'll be fun. Maybe we'll find a raccoon or something." I grabbed Lucas's arm to pull him, but he jerked away.

"No!" he declared. "Why're you always here? Why don't you stay on your side of the river?"

I looked at him sharply. "Why are you being so hateful? This ain't your river."

"More mine than it is yours," Lucas said. "Simon says white folks put up this fence, so white folks ought to stay on their own side of it. Simon says white folks are always gonna treat us like slaves, long as we let 'em. Simon says—"

"Simon says jump up and down. Simon says turn around," I declared hotly, mimicking the motions. "Simon says! What does Simon know, anyway?"

"He knows a lot!" Lucas's fists were clenched at his sides. I wondered if he aimed to take a punch at me. I readied myself to fight. "Simon knows more than you. He knows 'bout winnin' Negro folks their rights."

"What are you talking about?"

"Simon used to go travelin' with my daddy, gettin' Negroes to vote. Simon saw lots of things. He saw Daddy get shot."

Lucas looked at me, then quickly looked away, as if afraid of what he'd just said. I stared at him in surprise. "Your daddy got shot?"

Lucas studied the ground. He kicked a leaf with his foot. For a long time he didn't answer. "Folks said it was an accident," he said finally. "Simon and Daddy were in Georgia, pickin' up Negroes an' drivin' them to vote. We had a car then, so that was our job. There was some kind of fight an' a rifle went off." Lucas looked up at me. His eyes were watery. He swiped his nose with his hand. "Simon says it wasn't no accident."

I looked at Lucas in shocked disbelief. I once knew a boy whose daddy shot himself in a hunting accident, but I never knew anyone whose daddy was killed.

"Gosh, Lucas. I'm sorry, I—"

"Simon laid me out good for bringin' you to the house. Said I'd bring down calamity just as things are startin' to get movin'. Said I can't see you no more." Lucas glanced up at me, then quickly looked away. "Said he'll tan me if he catches me with you again."

"But . . ." I opened my mouth to protest. "But what

about the animals? I was going to help you with the animals. The ones you were gonna fix."

Lucas shrugged. His eyes looked sad. "I gotta go." He pulled up his trotline, then turned to walk away.

"Aren't you even gonna say good-bye?" I hollered. My voice cracked.

He raised a hand in farewell.

A knot rose in my throat. I had a funny kind of feeling as I watched Lucas disappear into the woods. A kind of strange, eerie stillness, like the way the air feels just before a tornado storm is about to hit. I shivered and turned to run home. I made it back just as Mama and Daddy were calling me for lunch.

chapter twelve

On Sunday morning a hot and clammy haze settled over Jericho. Daddy said the weather made his hands hurt. Said they remembered being younger and smaller and spending hours upon hours in the sun, picking cotton until they bled. He said he sure was glad he didn't have to survive by picking cotton anymore. I heard in school that some of the farm kids wouldn't come to classes until October, after the crop was in. I wondered if I could wait, and maybe make friends with some of them. They'd be outcasts, too, probably.

After opening announcements I trudged downstairs to Sunday school. Miss Hasty greeted me cheerily and pointed to the memory verse chart tacked on the wall. Every time we recited a memory verse, we got a gold star next to our name. Ten gold stars meant an announcement made in front of the entire congregation. I'd only been in town five weeks, but Miss Hasty sometimes asked me for two memory verses on the same day. The stars following my name hovered menacingly at nine. I slumped into my seat.

"I had so much fun at your party, Bobby Sue!" Martha Pierson flounced into the room and hovered next to Bobby Sue. I wrinkled my nose and started chewing the edge of my thumb. "Look! I still have a bruise where Tommy Parker pinched me."

"I can't believe those boys snuck into your party," Katie Moore said with a giggle.

Bobby Sue glanced at me. I buried my thumb in my lap and stared intently at the cover of my Bible. I tried not to care about Bobby Sue's party. Why didn't she like me, anyway? What did I ever do to her?

"Class! Class!" Miss Hasty clapped, calling us to order. Miss Hasty always looked excited about something. Even small things like a new piece of chalk got her praising God. She called it the joy of the Lord.

"We have something special happening today," she sang, pointing dramatically to the chart. "Josephine is going for her *tenth star.*"

I sank in my chair. Someone tittered.

"Ten stars? Wow, Josephine, what's next? The moon?" Bobby Sue asked. She said it sweet so Miss Hasty wouldn't know she was teasing, but I knew. I glared at the chart. The Bible said we could pray for anything and God would answer, but it wasn't true. Otherwise that chart would have exploded into a million pieces.

"Okay, Josephine, are you ready?" Miss Hasty clasped her hands in front of her and waited with a big smile on her face. Everyone in the room was waiting and watching so they could laugh at me.

My thumb snuck to my mouth. I gave it a couple of chews until Miss Hasty pursed her lips. I sighed and stood, ready to suffer the mortification of my tenth star. The verse was from St. Matthew, and I knew it backward and forward, but just as I was about to recite it I looked at Bobby Sue. She rolled her eyes. I had to do *something*. I couldn't go on letting her think I was a Bible-quoting Goody Two-shoes.

I opened my mouth. "If at first thou don't succeed, try, try again."

The room went silent for a minute, then someone giggled. Miss Hasty looked confused.

"Josephine, that's not our memory verse. I don't think that's even in the Bible."

My eyes darted to Bobby Sue. She looked curiously from me to Miss Hasty.

"It's not? Are you sure, Miss Hasty? I'm almost positive that's what you told us to memorize."

Miss Hasty looked flustered. Twin spots of red appeared on her cheeks. "Why, I'm certain it was St. Matthew. . . ." She picked up her Bible and began flipping the pages.

"I know a memory verse, too, Miss Hasty," said a voice in the back. A boy rose from his seat. "Early to bed and early to rise maketh a man healthy, wealthy, and wise." The class erupted in laughter. Another hand shot up, then another. Miss Hasty clapped. "Class! Class!" she called, but she couldn't get the class back to order. I sat down. Everyone thought it was comical, watching Miss Hasty get all ruffled and undone. I managed a bit of a grin at her antics, but I couldn't help feeling a little sorry for her. I knew what it felt like to get laughed at.

"That was funny, Jo." Bobby Sue caught up with me after class as I was climbing the stairs to church. "The way you got Miss Hasty so scattered. She even forgot to assign a memory verse for next week, did you notice?"

I nodded. "You really thought it was funny?"

"Yeah, the way you stood up there all serious like you were reciting a Bible verse, only it wasn't really." She shook her head. "I hate memorizing Bible verses. It's too hard. I can never seem to get them to stay in my head. I read the verse, but then—*poof!*—it's gone. But you were great today."

"Thanks." I felt a flush of triumph.

"Listen, I'm sorry about my party. I meant to invite you, but—"

"That's okay," I said quickly.

"Maybe you can come to the next one. Daddy said I could have a sleepover for my birthday."

A grin spread across my face. "A sleepover? That sounds like fun." I'd never been to a sleepover before. Daddy always said little girls belonged in their own beds at night. But I was older now. Old enough for a sleepover.

We reached the sanctuary. "Well, bye," Bobby Sue said. She went to sit with her parents.

I smiled. "Bye." I don't think I had ever been more excited in my entire life. Bobby Sue had talked to me and practically invited me to her birthday sleepover. I couldn't wait to tell Mama.

As I headed toward our pew, I saw Miss Hasty walk into the sanctuary. Her eyes looked red rimmed and puffy, and her face was pinched. I turned my eyes away and quickly sat down.

※

I fidgeted through Sunday dinner with the deacon chairman and his wife. They didn't seem to notice. The deacon chairman kept up a running conversation with Daddy about installing a new stained glass window in the vestibule, and his wife kept asking Mama, "Why is it that you are working, again, dear?" No one paid me any mind. As soon as they were gone I cleared the table without being asked, then escaped to my room. I was all mixed up inside. I couldn't tell if I felt happy about Bobby Sue or bad about Miss Hasty. I sank onto my bed and closed my eyes.

I must have napped because I woke to the sound of Mama and Daddy arguing. "What is it that you want, Maye?" I heard Daddy's voice through the walls. "Do you want me to get fired, is that it? Because that's what will happen. Claude Evans preached on the race issue in Columbia a few years back. He was barred from preaching in that church ever again. Folks around here aren't ready for that kind of . . . that kind of meddling in their affairs. And I'm not sure I blame them."

I crept to the door of my room so I could hear Mama's response.

". . . wouldn't be fitting for the preacher to meddle in people's affairs," she was saying with that dry edge to her voice.

"What do you want from me?" Daddy sounded angry. "You've been nudging and nagging since we moved down here. You want me to come right out and say colored folks ought to be allowed to eat alongside white folks, to go to school with our children, to take our jobs? Is that what you want?"

"I want you to do what you know is right and stop caring so much about what folks might think."

"You know, Maye, I've always loved your way of looking at life. But your . . . ideas . . . about how the world should work don't always fly. It's more complicated than that. Sometimes it's better for everyone to just do things the way they've always been done. No need to go off half-cocked trying to change the world. Especially when the world doesn't want changing."

"It's not the world, Joseph," Mama said softly. "It's one woman who wants to come to church."

"It's not that easy," Daddy protested. I crept farther into the hallway.

"Hello, Jo."

I jumped. I didn't know Mama could see me. I inched into the living room and tried to force a smile.

"Are you talking about Lenore Cooper?" I asked. I knew Mama had gone to visit her on more than one occasion. Rumors raced around town faster than Sheriff Overby's patrol car. "Why do you want her to come to church, Mama? People say she's bad." Praying for someone's soul at a camp revival meeting was one thing, but inviting her to church was something else entirely.

"Who told you she was bad?"

I shrugged. "Lots of folks." I didn't want Mama to invite Lenore Cooper to church. If people found out about it, there would be even more rumors and gossip. And Bobby Sue would never let me come to her sleepover.

"What did they say she did?" Mama asked.

I shrugged again, still not quite clear on that part of it. "She married a mulatto. And her little girl is mixed."

Mama nodded. "That's pretty much what she did."

"Why'd she do it, Mama?"

Mama sighed. "Same reasons other folks get married, I suppose."

Daddy sputtered. "And you aim to tell me that if Jo here up and decided to marry a Negro, it would be fine with you?"

I found a spot on the floor to study. He couldn't be

talking about me and Lucas. It wasn't like that. Not at all.

"Oh, Joseph!" Mama sounded exasperated. "That's so far beyond the point. I'm talking about common human decency. About fairness and loving your neighbor and all men being created equal. And if the preacher isn't the one to show that, then I don't know who is. You used to believe that. What's happened to you?"

"Nothing has happened. It's just . . . I was born here, Maye. I grew up here. I'm home now, and I'm finally respected, looked up to. I . . ." Daddy closed his mouth and shook his head.

Mama walked toward Daddy. She sat next to him and ran a finger down the strip of puckered red skin on the side of his face.

"Wounds heal, Joseph."

Daddy closed his eyes, then opened them again. "But they leave great big scars."

chapter thirteen

"Hey, Jo."

I glanced up from collecting my books and papers after school on Monday, startled to hear my name. Bobby Sue was standing next to my desk with a group of girls around her.

"We're going to the soda shop. Want to come?"

"Sure!" I declared.

"Okay. Let's go, then." Bobby Sue turned and strolled out of the classroom. I grabbed my things, then joined the girls. They were talking and laughing and flipping their hair. I bubbled with joy to be included.

Bobby Sue slid into a booth where the teenagers usually sat, and we piled in next to her. The soda jerk wiped his hands on his apron and walked over to take our order. I had twenty-five cents in my pocket that Mama had given me just that morning to buy some pecans for dinner. I fingered the money thoughtfully. The girls had all ordered and were staring at me.

"What'll it be?" the soda jerk asked.

I licked my lips. *I shouldn't get anything,* I told myself. *It's Mama's money.* But they were all waiting. A vanilla Coke would cost a dime. If I raced home and raced back, I could use my own money to buy the pecans. So it wasn't really taking Mama's money, so long as I was going to pay it back. I took a deep breath. "Vanilla Coke," I said. I closed my eyes and said a quick prayer.

"Look at this." Katie Moore pulled a silver tube out of her pocket. She took off the lid and twisted until a nub of red lipstick appeared. "It's Ravishing Red. Abigail gave it to me."

Katie had a sister in high school, which gave her special status.

"Wow," said Bobby Sue. "Have you tried it?"

"Not yet. I'm saving it for a special occasion." Katie twisted the tube until the lipstick disappeared.

I sipped on my vanilla Coke and tried to listen while the girls chattered about makeup and clothes and which boys were cute. I didn't much know what they were talking about. I wasn't allowed to wear makeup, and Mama always made all my clothes, and I didn't really care about boys except for wishing they'd finally give in and let me play stickball at recess. Those other topics seemed like important things to know about, though, at least to Bobby Sue and her friends, so I tried to pay attention and learn.

The door to the drugstore clanged open. I glanced up. Lucas Jefferson walked in with his little sister, LouEllen. My eyes widened and I quickly turned my head away, hoping they wouldn't see me. What if they said "hey" or asked me about the bump on my head? Then the other girls would know that I knew them.

The girls were chattering and not paying any attention. I peeked to see what Lucas and LouEllen were doing. Lucas was buying gauze and alcohol. I wondered if he had another sick animal. I felt a brief pang, wishing I could help. LouEllen stared toward the soda counter. She tugged on Lucas's arm. He shook his head, then marched across the drugstore toward the Colored line with his purchase.

"Hey, look," Bobby Sue said. "Isn't that the colored boy who was pulling you in that wagon last week? When you hurt your head?"

I froze. I didn't know what to say. I could feel the

flush creep up my neck. "I don't know," I said finally. "Maybe."

"It is!" Bobby Sue said decidedly. "I remember because of the way he walks."

I stared intently at my vanilla Coke and tried to think of something to change the subject. But my mind went blank. I hoped Lucas and LouEllen couldn't hear what we were saying.

"What's the matter with him?" Martha Pierson asked.

I shrugged.

"He walks like a pirate or something, with a wooden leg," Katie said.

"Call him Stump. Stump the colored pirate," Bobby Sue said, laughing. The girls started laughing with her. They looked at me, nudging me to join the joke. I peeked at Lucas, then at the girls I wanted to be my new friends. I opened my mouth and laughed, too, long and loud.

I glanced toward the door. Lucas's eyes met mine, then he turned away. I knew the minute I saw his face—he'd heard everything.

As soon as Lucas and LouEllen left the drugstore, I made an excuse that I had to go home. The vanilla Coke was sitting heavy on my stomach, and I thought I might be sick. I ran straight home and into my room.

It wasn't five minutes before Mama knocked on the door and asked me for the pecans. I mumbled something, hoping she would go away, but she didn't. She peeked in, then walked over to the bed.

"Did you buy the pecans?" she asked.

"No!" I retorted. I rolled over, half of me wishing Mama would go away and the other half wishing she would stroke my hair and tell me everything was okay.

"Why not, Josephine? Did something happen?"

"No."

"Then tell me why you are lying here on your bed instead of handing me either the pecans I asked you to get or the money I gave you to get them."

A sigh escaped from deep inside me. I wished I'd never met Lucas Jefferson.

Mama waited. It was the kind of wait that wasn't going anywhere until I talked.

"I don't like colored people," I blurted.

"Jo! Whatever do you mean?"

I swallowed the knot rising in my throat. "Why can't we just go back to Indiana, where folks were regular?" I'd never seen a Negro in Harrisburg, Indiana. Never.

Mama didn't say anything to that. She waited with her eyebrows furrowed and her mouth a straight line.

"Bobby Sue invited me to the soda shop after school," I said, thinking I ought to change the subject.

Mama nodded, still waiting.

"And I bought a vanilla Coke with the money."

"Oh, Jo!" Mama sounded disappointed. "I wish you would have asked me first. I wanted those pecans for dinner tonight."

"I'm sorry, Mama. I really am. I'll pay you back out of my piggy bank."

"Yes, you will."

"But I was having such a good time. We were talking about makeup and boys and stuff like that. Everyone was getting a Coke or a malted. We were sitting in a booth like the teenagers. I really wanted them to like me." The words rushed, one after the other.

"And that's what has you all upset?"

I gave a little half nod, half shrug. "Why do folks talk about Lenore Cooper so mean?" I asked.

Mama sat back on the bed and thought for a moment. Her eyes clouded. "I want to tell you a story. It's not a story about Lenore Cooper, it's about my grandmother." She looked at me. I nodded and she continued.

"Up until I was six years old, I thought my grandmother was the most wonderful woman on earth. Every Saturday I would go to her house and we would make arrowroot bread and tramp through the woods and hunt for mushrooms. She would tell me stories about the Great Coyote and how he tried to steal the moon. I thought she was beautiful, and I wanted to be just like her."

Mama sighed. "Then I went to school. Some of the kids laughed at me, because I had long black hair, like my grandmother. They called her a heathen and a savage, and said I must be one, too. Called me Squaw Baby and other names, worse names. I was so embarrassed and ashamed. One afternoon I went straight home from school, got my mother's sewing scissors, and cut off all my hair."

"Mama, you didn't!" I gasped.

Mama nodded. "That entire year I hated my grandmother. Hated her because she was an Indian, because her skin was red."

I sat wide-eyed, staring at Mama.

"Then, one afternoon I was riding through the woods when my horse spooked and threw me. I was bruised and scraped and scared. It was getting dark, and I was lost. It was Grandmother who found me. She washed my wounds in the creek, then carried me home on her back. I cried all the way. I didn't want to hate my grandmother. I loved her."

"What did you do?" I asked softly.

"I had a party," Mama said with a smile. "I invited all those kids to my grandmother's house. We built a campfire and caught fireflies and told stories. Not all the kids came, but some did. Once they got to know my grandmother, they stopped calling her those awful names. It didn't matter anymore that she was an Indian or that she looked different. Once they got to know her, they became her friends. And true friends don't treat each other mean, do they?" Mama stared at me when she asked that. It pierced me to the quick.

"No, Mama," I answered, and I knew that it was true.

I was setting the table for dinner and trying to get things sorted out in my mind when Daddy stormed into the house. His shoulders were tight and his head thrust forward. His eyes blazed angry. When he turned to me, I knew I'd done something. I wasn't sure quite what, but whatever it was, I was in some kind of trouble. I wanted to run and hide in a hole, but I couldn't. It was dinnertime.

Daddy waited until the food was served and grace was said before he let loose with what was bothering him. I started feeling prickly from just the way he looked at me. For a second I thought he was mad because he'd heard that I had laughed at Lucas.

"Yancy Hasty stopped by my office today," Daddy said finally. "He told me what happened. Do you have anything to say for yourself, Jo?"

I tried to make the connection, to figure out what Daddy was talking about. He couldn't mean what happened at the soda shop, so it had to be something else. Yancy Hasty. He owned the service station, had a wife and two little babies, and was the brother to Miss Hasty. Uh-oh.

"I'm sorry," I mumbled. I bowed my head.

"I am so ashamed," Daddy said. He told Mama what I had done in Sunday school and how the rest of the students had followed my lead. Mama's face fell with disappointment. I flinched. I hated that look worse than any spanking. It made me feel low-down and mean.

"Miss Hasty is a loyal and dedicated teacher, and you've made her question her ability to lead your class. How could you, Jo?"

I didn't know how to respond to that, except to do my usual shrug.

"The Good Lord knows we won't find anyone else to teach the sixth graders," Daddy said. He attacked his butter beans, then resumed his tirade.

"Since you seem to be hung up on Scripture memorization, I'm going to give you an extra passage to recite in front of the Sunday schools next week. All of them. I'll come down personally to make sure you do it right."

"Daddy!" I couldn't believe he was doing this. "The other kids . . ." I looked to Mama for support, but she seemed to be in full agreement. "But . . ."

"No arguments, Jo. You will do it, and you'll do it with a smile on your face. And you will, of course, apologize to Miss Hasty."

I didn't say anything. I just stared angrily at my plate. I was going to look like some kind of fool parading around to all the Sunday school classes. I'd get laughed clear out of Jericho.

"Hard day, Joseph?" Mama asked.

"That isn't the half of it," Daddy said. He jabbed into his mashed potatoes. "Everyone has an opinion or a suggestion or a notion that they've been duly appointed as God's spokesperson for my betterment. If it wasn't my sermon, it was my tie or the way I read the Scripture or the closing hymn. Then I had to hear all about Josephine's antics."

Daddy's jaw twitched angrily. He speared a pork chop and twisted it on the plate. Then he looked up at Mama.

"You went to visit Obadiah Jenkins again, didn't you?"

"I took him a pair of reading glasses that I found in the Missionary Aid box," Mama said. She looked straight back at Daddy. "His sight is failing him. The poor man only wants to read his Bible."

I looked from Mama to Daddy, relieved the attention had been shifted away from me. I had never heard of Obadiah Jenkins. He didn't go to our church. Maybe he was a Methodist.

"He has his own people to take care of him. We talked about this, Maye. You can't be going alone into the home of a widowed Negro man. It's unseemly. That's how rumors get started."

I drew back and studied Mama.

"He is eighty years old!" Mama retorted. "And he is dying. If a pair of reading glasses will ease him through this life, then who am I to deny him that? I thought . . ." Mama turned away and closed her eyes. She exhaled and turned back to Daddy. "I thought you'd at least support me in this."

"It's just that people are talking, Maye. Wondering why you can't concentrate your visits to the sick and shut-in of First Baptist."

"I go visiting every week, to *whomever* needs comfort or encouragement or prayer, just the same as I've always done in Indiana and Ohio and Tennessee before that. Now all of a sudden everyone is taking an interest?"

"Everything we do is of interest," Daddy said.

I knew that was true.

"Well, good," Mama said with a firm set to her jaw. "Now maybe things will get interesting."

Daddy sighed, and I knew that he had just lost whatever battle they had been fighting. "The deacons have called a special meeting on Thursday evening," he said.

Mama nodded. She resumed eating as if nothing had happened. "I have a Ladies' Circle meeting on Thursday," she said. "I'll have Abilene make up some desserts. Jo can serve."

I started to protest. Deacons' meetings filled me with dread. They were long and boring and they most always resulted in somebody telling Daddy how I'd been misbehaving in some way or another. Then I saw the look on Daddy's face and I closed my mouth. I was already in enough trouble.

chapter fourteen

Bobby Sue sat with me at lunch on Tuesday, and she let me join her circle of friends during recess to whisper and gossip and share secrets. I should have been the happiest girl in the world. But I still couldn't shake the nagging feeling of guilt.

After school Bobby Sue invited me to the soda shop again. She had a pocketful of change and was going to play "Teddy Bear," the new song by Elvis, over and over on the jukebox. But I couldn't go. Mama said the soda shop was off-limits the rest of the week because I had used her money without asking.

Bobby Sue pouted when I told her I couldn't go. "Suit yourself," she said. She flounced away with her friends. I was forced to walk home alone. Some days it seemed nothing could go right.

Abilene was scrubbing dishes, up to her elbows in soapy water, when I came inside.

"Afternoon, Miss Jo," she said.

"Hello, Miz Abilene." I threw my books on the kitchen table and studied her. Lucas probably hated me, I thought. I wondered if he had told Abilene what I'd done. I hoped not. I didn't want her to know what an awful person I was.

Miz Abilene caught my eye and tossed me a dish towel. I was careful to catch it. A dropped dish towel brought either bad luck or unwanted visitors, according to Abilene. "You can help me dry," she declared.

I stood next to her and dried the dishes as she handed them to me. She hummed while she worked. Outside, the mockingbird whistled *teel-a-weet, teel-a-weet*. It was a song he sang over and over again. Mama called it "Variations on a Sparrow."

"That old bird," Abilene said. "Mighty racket, that one. Must know the song of every bird here'bouts."

I glanced outside. The mockingbird perched on a branch, beak open wide.

"Does he always just copy?" I said aloud. "Does he ever sing his own song?"

Abilene paused. "I heard tell that every now an' then a mockingbird will work up the courage to sing his own. But you'd be mighty blessed to hear it."

I dried the last dish and put it in the cupboard. The mockingbird cut short his song and flew to a lower branch. Abilene started dinner. I knew from the past that I only got in her way and annoyed her when she was trying to cook, so I scooted outside.

I wandered around the house. I itched to go to the river, but Lucas wouldn't want to see me. And I didn't feel like facing him. I picked up a rock and chucked it. I figured I'd just stick around the house and feel sorry for myself.

I picked up another rock and threw it as hard as I could. *The boys should let me play stickball,* I told myself as I watched the rock whiz through the air toward the tree.

Suddenly I heard a horrible screech, then something fluttered to the ground.

It took a moment to realize what I'd done, then I ran, crying, toward the tree. The mockingbird lay in a mess of feathers on the ground. I carefully picked him up and cradled him in my hand.

"Abilene! Abilene!" I cried.

Abilene came rushing out the back door.

"What is it, child?"

I showed her the bird. "I didn't mean to," I sobbed.

Abilene clucked her tongue. She reached toward the bird with her large, brown hands and smoothed back the feathers. "Bruised wing," she said. "And scared half to death." She looked pained. "I'm sorry, chile. That poor bird's hurt pretty bad."

She looked at me with sorrowful eyes. I stared down at the bird. I could see his heartbeat flutter in his throat. His dark eyes blinked, and he let out a low, mournful whistle.

I held the bird close to my chest and ran for the woods.

"Lucas! Lucas!" I screamed as I tore through the brambles into the clearing. "Lucas!" He just had to be there. The mockingbird had its beak open and was breathing in shallow, gasping pants. "Lucas!"

I sank to my knees in the tall grass and started to pray. I didn't know what else to do.

I felt him before I saw him. I looked up and there was Lucas peering at me from behind a thorn bush, a look of anger on his face.

"What're you doin' here?" he asked.

I showed him the bird. "I hit him. With a rock. I didn't mean to. It was an accident. Can you help him? Please?" Tears rolled down my face and dripped off the end of my nose, but I couldn't wipe them away.

Lucas looked suspicious, but he approached. He gently took the bird out of my hands. "A mocking-bird," he said. He ran a finger over the bird's head and the underside of his beak and along the wing. The bird clicked his beak shut, then opened it again in what looked like a silent scream.

"Don't know much 'bout birds," he said. "Their wings are mighty delicate." He paused. "But I'll try."

I sighed and felt a huge burden lift off me. If anybody could fix that bird, Lucas could.

I woke early the next morning and stopped by the clearing on the way to school. Lucas was already there. The night before we had built a cage out of reeds and twigs and set it off the ground to keep the mockingbird safe and contained. Lucas had wrapped the wing in a crude sort of splint he plastered with herbs. We gathered sunflower seeds and berries and water so the bird could eat and drink during the day. Then we each went our separate ways—Lucas to his school and me to mine.

The school day moved in slow motion. I could hardly keep my mind on my work what with worry about the bird and how he was faring.

"Hey, Jo." Bobby Sue approached my desk after the last bell rang. "I have to go to the library after school to pick up a book for my daddy." She made a face. "Want to come with me?"

"Sure!" I replied quickly. Mama hadn't said anything

about me not being able to go to the library. I was glad to be invited. I was afraid Bobby Sue would forget about being my friend since I wasn't allowed at the soda shop. Then I shook my head. The mockingbird. I needed to check on the mockingbird.

"Oh, no," I said. "I can't go."

Bobby Sue frowned. "Why not?"

"Well, there's this bird. . . ."

"A bird?"

I nodded. "A mockingbird." I wanted to tell Bobby Sue all about the hurt bird and how Lucas was fixing it. But something stopped me. I looked at Bobby Sue. She crossed her arms and waited for my decision.

"Never mind." I shook my head. "I'll go with you." Bobby Sue smiled, and I knew she wasn't mad at me. I'd visit the mockingbird as soon as we were done at the library.

The library was hushed and drowsy. Bobby Sue went straight to the desk to get the book for her daddy. I browsed through the stacks, pulling out books and flipping through them to see if there were some I wanted to read. I stretched and inhaled the library smells. I decided that the library was the most peaceful place in the world, except for church after all the people had gone home.

Bobby Sue was waiting for me at the desk. I was walking toward her with my arms filled when I saw something that made my heart stop. It was a book, brand-new and crackling, like it had never been opened. The title said *Songbirds,* written by the National Audubon Society. I opened the book and flipped the pages until I saw a full-color picture of a mockingbird, wings outstretched. I snapped the book shut.

My head quickly filled with wild thoughts. What I was thinking would cause me nothing but trouble if Bobby Sue found out, but I couldn't stop myself.

"Are you ready?" Bobby Sue asked.

I nodded. Quickly, so as not to think about it too much, I stuck the book on the bottom of my stack. I felt like I had only half my breath. It wasn't like I was doing anything wrong, I told myself. Just checking out some books. I counted to make sure I didn't have too many. Four books, that's what I had. Four was the limit. Maybe I should only get three, so Bobby Sue wouldn't ask why I read so much. But Miss Spinnaker knew I checked out four books every two weeks. Only having three might seem strange. I debated back and forth.

"Let's go," Bobby Sue said.

My mouth tasted like cotton. I took my stack to the desk. "I'd like to check these out," I said to Miss Spinnaker. "Please." My voice trembled. I told myself to stop being so scared. After all, no one could jump into my head and know I was thinking of giving one of those books to Lucas. Could they? I looked at the countertop and listened to my heart thump.

Miss Spinnaker stamped the cards and slid them into the pockets of the books. Thump-swish, thump-swish.

"Stand up straight, Josephine, dear, with your head held high. You must carry yourself as befitting your station as the daughter of a preacher. It's an important responsibility you have, as your father is in the service of God. His is a most elevated calling, you know."

Miss Spinnaker was one of the devout, never missing a church service—Sundays, Wednesdays, or otherwise. Like other devouts I had met, she felt it her beholden responsibility to train me up properly in my Christian duty. I blushed and risked a glance at Bobby Sue. She rolled her eyes. I grinned.

"That's lovely," Miss Spinnaker said. "One can always tell a Christian by their manner of walking—tall and proud and devoted to service. Don't you agree?"

"Yes'm," I mumbled.

"Speak up, dear. The elect must always speak with clarity and force. That's one thing I admire about your father. He has his faults, of course, that God will work out of him in His own time, but your father always—"

"Thank you, ma'am," I said, grabbing the books. "I'll tell him you said so."

I cradled the books. Bobby Sue and I raced outside. I'd done it. I'd gotten the book! All I had to do was make it to the clearing without anyone getting suspicious.

"Stand up straight, dear," Bobby Sue mimicked in a high, squeaky voice as we walked down the sidewalk. "One can always tell a Christian by their manner of walking." She swung her hips and twisted her shoulders.

"Speak up, dear," I said in the same squeaky voice. "The elect always speak with clarity and force."

"Of course, dear!" Bobby Sue yelled. "I most agree!"

We laughed. I thought that maybe I could tell Bobby Sue about Lucas.

"There's Sheriff Overby," Bobby Sue said. I looked and saw the sheriff polishing the windows of the courthouse. He caught our reflection in a window, turned, and waved. I waved back.

"He's such a goof," Bobby Sue said.

I took another glance at the sheriff. I thought he seemed nice.

"Daddy says he's much too lenient and should have never been elected. He wouldn't do a thing about Lenore Cooper's husband. Daddy says it's because he's soft on coloreds."

I decided then and there that I would never mention a thing about Lucas to Bobby Sue.

I talked Bobby Sue into going straight home and giving her daddy that book. That way she would get on his good side and he'd be sure to let her have that sleepover party. Bobby Sue agreed. "Good thinking."

As soon as she was safely out of sight, I cut out and raced for the woods. I reached the clearing in record time.

The bird! I searched the bushes where Lucas and I had built the cage. I raced around the clearing, my eyes scanning every bush and corner. Nothing. No Lucas, no bird. Something awful must have happened. I knew I should have come straight here after school. Now the bird was gone and it was all my fault.

"What're you doin'?" Lucas walked up behind me. I whirled around.

"The mockingbird," I said. "It's gone! What if a raccoon got it, or . . ."

Lucas held out his hands. The bird was nestled snugly between them.

"Crazy bird's been tryin' to fly out of the cage. I gotta fix it, but I can't do that and keep the bird still, too. Here, you hold 'im."

I took the bird in my hands and watched while Lucas

wove more reeds into the cage to make it stronger. "Is he any better?" I asked. The bird was a soft, warm weight in my hands. I could feel the beating of his heart.

Lucas shrugged. "He ain't pantin' so much, but he didn't eat none of the seeds or berries. I counted 'em."

"Has he sung?" Somehow, I thought that if the bird would just sing again, that would mean he was going to be all right.

Lucas shook his head.

He took the mockingbird, rewrapped his wing, then put him back into the cage for the evening. The bird looked back at us with those dark, dark eyes.

Lucas turned away. We still hadn't said anything about what had happened at the soda shop.

"I got you something," I blurted before I lost my courage.

I held the book toward him, spanning the distance between us. "I saw it at the library. Thought it might help. With the bird and everything."

Lucas took the book and held it gingerly, like it might break. "For me?"

"Not to keep," I said. "Just to borrow. I have to have it back in two weeks."

Lucas studied the book, his eyes wide as saucers. Then he looked up at me. "Why are you doing this?"

I shrugged, feeling embarrassed. "I thought it would help you learn about the bird."

"Simon won't like this." Lucas turned the book over and over in his hands.

"Why not?"

"Negroes ain't allowed at the library, and we ain't got one of our own."

"That's why I checked it out for you," I said slowly, in case he didn't understand. If he could have gotten the library book for himself, I wouldn't have gone to the trouble. "Just read it and get it back to me. Simon doesn't have to know."

Lucas nodded. "Right." He clutched the book under his arm and grinned. "Let's go, Moses." Lucas took off running in that galloping way of his. Then he stopped and waved. "Thanks, Jo!"

I smiled and waved back. I knew that what I'd done in the soda shop had been wrong, but somehow I felt forgiven.

chapter fifteen

I wasn't able to play with Bobby Sue or to see about Lucas and the mockingbird on Thursday after school. It was the night of the deacons' meeting. Daddy wanted me straight home. He was as nervous as a cat in a dogfight.

Daddy wore his best blue suit and a burgundy tie, even though it wasn't Sunday. He fiddled and muttered and pulled at the tie until I came over and got the knot right. When I was in third grade, we lived in a town on the Ohio River and Jake Riley, the ferryman, taught me all about tying knots. Daddy's shoes were polished and his shirt was starched and he looked near perfect, except, of course, for the scar.

Abilene served us a quiet dinner, then left for home. I straightened up in the kitchen and checked on the desserts, then escaped to my room to do homework. Daddy's restlessness grated like fingernails on a chalk-board.

I huddled at the desk in my room and tried to concentrate on learning the nine rules for the use of capital letters. I heard a knock at the door, followed by forced greetings and solemn hellos as the men gathered in the living room. Deacons always seemed to be an especially somber group of people, at least when they gathered in groups. Maybe it was on account of trying to handle so much of God's business.

The first part of the meeting droned on with attendance and minutes and talk about the budget. Offerings were up, which was sure to please Daddy. Someone brought up hymn selection, which caused a little row, but Daddy smoothed it over. Every church Daddy'd ever preached, as long as I could remember, had fights about music. What songs to sing, what songs not to sing, how fast to sing them, organ or piano. Daddy was well practiced at settling those arguments. All in all, the meeting seemed to be going pretty well, at least from my listening post. I thought perhaps Daddy could relax.

"Let's get to the real reason we called this meeting," someone said. I tilted my head to listen. It was a voice I didn't recognize. "Frankly, we are concerned about

Maye. She isn't behaving appropriately, as the preacher's wife."

They were talking about Mama. I bristled at the comment.

"We are afraid," said a voice I did know, Yancy Hasty's, "that she is serving as a bad influence on her daughter. Your daughter."

A bad influence!

"A bad influence?" Daddy sputtered.

"Look at it from our vantage point," said another voice. "She is working outside the home at a job that is, frankly, questionable; she has hired Abilene Jefferson, whose husband was known to be uppity, to watch over Josephine; and she keeps company with some rather unsavory characters."

I narrowed my eyes. *How dare they talk that way about Abilene!* She wasn't uppity. I wasn't entirely clear on what that meant, but it sure sounded bad.

"Unsavory characters?" Daddy asked. His voice sounded low, almost a growl. I thought he must be getting angry.

"Treva Lane, her boss, for one. Treva is a borderline Christian. She certainly doesn't attend church every Sunday. Then there are rumors that Maye has, ahem, gone visiting with the likes of Lenore Cooper."

I cringed. What would Daddy say to that?

"What's more," the man continued, "she visited Obadiah Jenkins in his home. In the colored quarters. And him in bed!"

"She leads the ministry to the sick and shut-in!" Daddy argued. "It's her Christian duty!"

I nodded. *Tell 'em, Daddy.* I didn't want anyone talking bad about Mama.

"The coloreds have their own churches, their own people to care for the sick," said Yancy Hasty. "There is a certain decorum that needs to be respected. We wouldn't want the Negroes to get the wrong idea. We must protect our way of life."

"But of course," Daddy said. He had an ominous edge to his voice. Once at a deacons' meeting in Harrisburg, his face turned purple and a vein started throbbing in his forehead, he was that mad. I wished I could sneak out and see what was happening.

"Our coloreds are happy with the way things are," another voice said. "There's no use stirring things up and putting ideas in their heads, which is what your wife is doing."

"Ideas?" Daddy asked.

"Separate but equal," someone said in a loud voice. "That's the way it should be and always will be. Why, we lose that and we lose everything. Next thing you know, Negroes will be taking our jobs, buying our homes, even marrying our women.

"Think about your own daughter, Reverend. She *has* been seen keeping company with a colored boy, your maid's boy. I think you might want to look to your own interests."

I leapt to my feet, fists clenched. Daddy was saying something, but I didn't hear him because the blood was pounding so hot in my ears. Then Daddy called my name to serve coffee and dessert. I took several deep breaths, counted to ten. Then I walked into that room with my head high. I carried Mama's silver tray filled with canapés and scuppernong tarts and tried to pass it without hurling the food into anyone's face. I was madder than sin.

The men ate the tarts and drank the coffee and settled back in their chairs. Everyone looked pleasant and relaxed. Everyone but Daddy, who looked ready to spit nails.

"I understand you are memorizing Scripture for recitation this Sunday," Yancy Hasty said, loud enough for everyone to hear.

"Yes, sir," I muttered. I studied the ground. My impending humiliation was his fault. He shouldn't have told Daddy what I had done.

"Why don't you recite for us, Josephine?" Mr. Snyder

said. From the sound of his voice I knew he was the one who had told everyone I'd been seen with Lucas. I glared at him.

"I wouldn't want to disturb your meeting," I replied through clenched teeth.

"It wouldn't be a disturbance," Mr. Snyder insisted. "It's always a pleasure to hear children recite the Good Book."

"No, really . . ." I looked at Daddy with pleading in my eyes.

Daddy wasn't paying me any mind. His jaw twitched and his eyes wore a far-off look. He glanced at me suddenly, as if just realizing I was there.

"Go ahead, Jo," he said.

I looked around at those men, still feeling the anger boil in me, and had a flash of brilliance. Daddy had told me to memorize the Sermon on the Mount, but for these men I was going to recite something else, the wickedest verses I knew of in the whole New Testament. I took a deep breath.

"Woe unto you, scribes and Pharisees, hypocrites! for ye compass sea and land to make one proselyte, and when he is made, ye make him twofold more the child of hell than yourselves. . . . Ye serpents, ye generation of vipers, how can ye escape the damnation of hell?" My cheeks burned. I put every ounce of feeling I had into those verses. Mr. Snyder pressed his lips together in a thin, bloodless line. Yancy Hasty sat stiff with wide, unblinking eyes. Daddy was making a snuffling sound and holding his chin.

"Thank you, Jo," Daddy said when I'd finished. His voice cracked. "You may clear now, please." He turned to the men. "I think that concludes our meeting. Thank you for coming, gentlemen. I will take your suggestions to heart. Let us close with prayer."

I fiddled in the kitchen while Daddy prayed, alternately chewing my thumb and rinsing dessert plates. I wondered what he was going to do with me. I'd probably be banished to my room for a year, or made to read the Bible cover to cover, or forced to recite Scripture every Sunday until I died. I straightened my shoulders and determined to take my punishment without a whimper. It had been worth it.

After the prayer the men gathered their things and bustled out the door with hardly a word. No one looked at me. When they were gone, Daddy leaned on the edge of the kitchen door frame. I busied myself with the dishes.

"I didn't realize you had memorized that passage," he said finally.

"Yes, sir." I had learned it on my own because it was naughty and had so many bad words.

"Quite a recap to our meeting."

"Yes, sir." I forced my eyes to meet Daddy's. Might as well face my punishment, get it over with.

"Many's the time I wanted to quote those particular verses to certain individuals." Daddy nodded slowly. "You taught me something tonight."

I glanced at Daddy in surprise. "You're not mad?"

"Oh, I'm mad," he said. "But not at you."

"At Mama?" I was ready to defend Mama.

"No. Not at your mama."

I couldn't figure who it was that made Daddy mad. "Abilene is *not* uppity," I declared. I didn't want Daddy to fire her on account of what those men said. If she didn't have a job, then Lucas and LouEllen might have to quit school and go pick cotton.

"Abilene's fine."

"Then it's the deacons," I confirmed smugly. It had to be them. Those men sure deserved Daddy's anger, saying what they had.

Daddy sighed and shook his head. "They were only repeating what they've heard from others before them. No one's ever taught them any different."

"Then who are you mad at?" I watched Daddy's face intently, studying the set of his jaw and the twisting path the scar took down his face.

"At me, Jo. I'm mad at me."

chapter sixteen

That Sunday I had to recite Scripture for all the Sunday schools, starting with the little four-year-olds and working up to the high schoolers. I was paraded about like a show pony. It was humiliating. But Bobby Sue Snyder had overheard her dad talking about what I'd done at the deacons' meeting, and she told all her friends. They asked me if I would help them learn the same passage and any others I knew with bad words. I was a celebrity, which made it not so awful.

I spent the next week trying to shuffle between Bobby Sue and Lucas. Bobby Sue was a hard one to stay friends with sometimes. She got mad if I couldn't go with her to the soda shop or the five-and-ten. She'd walk off in a huff and wouldn't speak to me again until I apologized, which I thought was unfair. But if I didn't apologize, then I was back to having no friends because everyone followed the lead of Bobby Sue.

At the same time, the mockingbird was quickly getting better. He was starting to eat and flex his wing. He still hadn't sung a note, but I was sure he would soon. Lucas said it was nearly time to release him. I didn't want to miss that.

On Thursday afternoon Bobby Sue had to go to Greenville with her mama, so after school I struck out for the woods. The ground was muddy, so I wore my yellow boots, which made my feet sweat. I tried to sneak out without them, but Abilene caught me and made me put them on. She didn't ask me where I was going, just said to keep myself clean and out of trouble. I never could tell her about the time I spent with Lucas. That seemed the kind of thing that would get her looking worried and worn, like when she would talk about Simon and what he would do for a job after the cotton got picked.

When I reached the woods at the edge of the fence, Lucas was waiting. He grinned when he saw me and pulled a newspaper-wrapped bundle from out of his shirt. It was the book I'd loaned him.

"The book shore helped," he said. "I think the bird's ready to fly."

"Hooray!" I raised my arm in triumph. "Let's go."

We raced to the clearing. The mockingbird was in his cage, his wing bandaged with gauze. Lucas reached inside and gathered the bird in his hands. I watched as he gently unwrapped the wing and set the bird on the ground. I was going to miss taking care of him. The mockingbird had been in Lucas's care for over a week.

The bird turned his head, eyes darting toward us, then away. He hopped forward and turned his head again.

"Is he gonna fly?" I whispered. I crossed my fingers and prayed.

Lucas nodded. "He's just gettin' a feel for his freedom."

The bird hopped again. He ruffled his feathers and smoothed them down. Then he took two quick jumps, stretched his wings, and flapped into the air.

"He's flying!" I hollered. Lucas whooped. We watched the mockingbird soar into the sky.

"Reckon he remembers his way home?" I was suddenly fearful that after spending so much time in a cage the bird would forget where he'd built his nest. "Maybe we should have released him closer."

"He'll remember."

"Think he'll sing again?" I hadn't heard a peep out of the bird since I'd injured him. I missed his raucous singing outside my window.

"One day." Lucas handed me the book. "Thanks." He smiled shyly. "Think you can get me another one?" he asked. "Simon says there's a need for Negro doctors. Maybe I could learn 'bout fixin' humans from those books. An anatomy book, maybe?"

"I guess I could look for something," I said. I hoped that whatever I did find didn't have any naked pictures. Miss Spinnaker would surely get to preaching at me were I to check out a book like that. And what would Bobby Sue think?

Lucas stared at me, a serious look on his face. "What you're doing is like civil disobedience."

"What?"

"Civil disobedience. You know. When a person stands against something that's wrong. Like when those colored folks in Montgomery wouldn't ride the buses till things were fair."

Mama had told me about Montgomery, Alabama, way back in February, when Dr. Martin Luther King, Jr., was on the cover of *Time* magazine, before I had ever met a Negro. She had read about Mrs. Rosa Parks, who wouldn't give up her seat on the bus. Mama'd said things were starting to change.

I shook my head. "Checking out books in the library ain't the same as that."

"Shore is. A bit."

I shook my head again. "Can't be civil disobedience, on account of it's secret. And it's gonna stay secret, right?" I glared at Lucas. I felt trembly at the thought that someone might find out what I was doing.

"I reckon."

"It had better stay a secret, Lucas Jefferson, or else . . ." I thought for a minute. "Or else Simon will tan you silly."

Lucas frowned. Then he shrugged. "Anyway, it's civil disobedience 'tween me and you."

"That doesn't count," I said.

"That's what you say." Lucas's face looked stubborn. "But I say it's somethin'. And maybe you'll get caught." His voice brightened, like that would be a good thing.

"That'd be awful!" My stomach did a funny little flip. "I don't want to get caught!"

"Simon says when the time comes, that folks got to be ready to stand down injustice. Go to jail, even."

"Jail!" My eyes grew wide at the thought. I decided that I couldn't get any more books for Lucas. Not if it meant I might get caught. Folks would talk something terrible. No, I couldn't do any more civil disobedience.

Then I looked at Lucas. A knot rose in my throat.

Lucas needed those books so he could keep learning how to fix things.

I took the newspaper-wrapped book and gave a little wave. Then I trudged home through the woods, wishing I could figure a way out of this whole mess.

I stayed away from the woods the rest of the week and spent all my time at the soda shop with Bobby Sue and her friends. We played "All Shook Up" on the jukebox, and I used the last of my money on vanilla Cokes. I missed the river and the trees, but I didn't want to risk seeing Lucas. I couldn't bear for him to ask if I'd gotten another book.

The mockingbird never came home. I searched everywhere, all around the tree, but there was no sign of him. Maybe that wing wasn't strong enough to fly after all. I was scared that the next time I went to the woods I'd find him dead on the ground.

On Tuesday morning Bobby Sue burst into class, excitement bouncing off her like waves. She wouldn't say why, though. Just shook her head and grinned. After class we gathered around her as she passed out envelopes to every girl in the sixth grade.

I slid open the envelope with my finger and pulled out a sheet of fancy white paper.

"It's an invitation to my sleepover party," Bobby Sue declared before I had a chance to read the writing. Everyone oohed and aahed. Bobby Sue smiled even wider. "It's on Friday night, at my house. We're going to have cake and ice cream and play games and listen to my brand-new record player."

"You got a record player?" one of the girls asked.

"I'm getting one, for my birthday."

I smiled and pocketed the invitation in my book bag, taking care to keep it dry and clean. A sleepover! I waved good-bye to the girls and hurried to ask Mama if I could go.

I passed the library on my way home. I paused in front of the steps, then made a quick decision. I would get Lucas one more book, only one, and that would be it. Then I would give up the river and Lucas forever. I had to make a choice. I decided that being friends with Bobby Sue and the other girls was the most important thing.

I browsed through the library stacks and finally found a book titled *Gray's Anatomy*, a thick book the size of an encyclopedia. I blushed when Miss Spinnaker checked it out. She didn't say anything, though, just raised her eyebrows and looked me up and down.

I walked to the river, trying to figure out how to tell Lucas I couldn't keep seeing him. I tried not to think about the mockingbird. When I got to the fence, Lucas was there with Moses.

"The mockingbird's gone," I announced. As soon as I said it I felt tears well in my eyes. I blinked and bit my lower lip to try and push them back.

"He's all right. I seen him th' other day, flyin' about the clearing."

"You did?" I stared at Lucas. "Why hasn't he come back to his tree, then?"

Lucas shrugged. "He will."

I looked at him, wondering if he was telling the truth. I was still worried. It was eerie, not having the mockingbird around the house. "Has he sung?" I asked.

Lucas shook his head.

I sighed, then pulled the book out of my bag and handed it to Lucas. He looked it over eagerly, then wrapped it in a piece of newspaper and stuck it under the bib in his overalls. I opened my mouth to tell him that it was the last one I would get for him, but he interrupted me.

"If I tell you somethin', will you promise not to tell no one till it's over and done?"

"What?" I asked. I was starting to feel grumpy. The mockingbird was gone, this was probably my last time in the woods, and Lucas wouldn't let me say what I needed to say.

"You promise?"

"Yes. I promise already."

"I ain't gonna need you to get me books no more."

I felt a surge of relief. This was perfect, like a sign sent from God.

"Really?" I tried to keep the excitement out of my voice.

"I told Simon what you did. Gettin' me that book so I could help the bird and all."

"You told Simon? Why'd you go and do a thing like that?" Anger replaced relief. I couldn't believe it. Lucas was going to ruin everything. "What did he say?"

"Simon said it wasn't right, you gettin' me books like that."

"Course he did! You knew he'd say that all along. You shouldn't have told him." I was so mad, I wanted to rip *Gray's Anatomy* away from him and throw it to the ground. "What will he do?"

"He said we're gonna integrate the library."

"You're what?"

"Integrate the library. Friday, after school. Simon's gonna cut off pickin' early, and we're plannin' to get me a library card."

"Have you gone plumb crazy?"

"I'm not crazy," Lucas announced. "Simon says it ain't fair Negroes don't have a library of our own. He says it's time to take a stand. Civil disobedience."

"It can't be civil disobedience," I declared. I stomped my foot, scared about what I'd started, about what might happen when Lucas stepped foot in that library. "You promised it'd stay secret."

Lucas shrugged. "Simon says . . ."

"Oh, shut up about Simon!"

Lucas looked me up and down. "Are you gonna tell?"

"No," I said, angry at myself and angry at Lucas. "*I'm* not a tattle." I turned and marched out of the woods, determined to never see Lucas again.

chapter seventeen

Mama said I could go to Bobby Sue's party. She even offered to make me a party dress, but I said no. I didn't want a party dress. Every time I thought about the party and about Friday night, a terrible feeling came over me. Bobby Sue's party meant everything to me, so why couldn't I feel happy?

I stayed away from the river. I didn't want to worry about the mockingbird. I didn't go anywhere near the fence or the woods, afraid I might meet up with Lucas. Mostly I came straight home after school. I shadowed Abilene, wanting to ask her if she knew what Lucas was about to do but keeping my mouth shut because I had promised not to tattle.

That night the radio news announced that President Eisenhower sent the 101st Airborne to Little Rock,

Arkansas, so nine Negro children could go to an all-white high school. Mama whooped when she heard it. Daddy raised his eyebrows. "The 101st Airborne," he mused. I thought he was going to launch into a story about the war, but he didn't. He looked at Mama. "It's a battleground now."

Mama nodded. "It's a war."

I looked from Mama to Daddy, trying to read what was passing between them. "Why do those kids want to go to that school?" I asked.

"Because it's right," Mama said. "And because those nine kids have the courage to light the way."

"But if it's right," I said, pondering what I wanted to ask, "then why is it so important to folks that Negroes stay separate?" I was thinking of the water fountains, and the library, and the fence around the Quarters.

"Because of fear," Daddy said suddenly.

I wondered if President Eisenhower would need to send the army to Jericho.

On Friday, I walked to school slowly. When I reached the fork in the road, I looked toward the fence, then turned away quickly. Butterflies banged about in my stomach. I felt so on edge that I could hardly stay in my seat during morning classes. Mrs. Millhouse called on me twice to stop fidgeting and said if I couldn't sit still, she'd hold me after school. When the bell rang for lunch, I nearly flew out of my seat.

"You going to sit with us, Josephine?" Bobby Sue asked as I was halfway out the classroom door.

I skidded to a stop and nodded. "Sure," I said. I bounced on my toes and chewed my thumb, waiting for the rest of the girls to gather their lunches and get in line.

"I am so excited about your party, Bobby Sue," one of the girls chattered as we filed to the lunchroom.

Bobby Sue smiled. "You should be," she said. "Mother's had the colored help cooking and cleaning for days. You've never been inside my house, have you, Jo?"

I shook my head no. I'd only seen their white-pillared mansion from the road.

"You're going to love it," Katie Moore said. She swapped her ham-and-cheese sandwich with Martha Pierson for an apple turnover.

"Just don't get in any more trouble," Bobby Sue warned. "You don't want Mrs. Millhouse to make you stay after."

I nodded and took a bite of my chicken sandwich,

letting the girls think I was fidgeting in class because I was excited about the party.

That wasn't the truth, though. I was fidgeting because I was nervous about Lucas and what he aimed to do this afternoon. I wasn't sure if I was nervous for his sake or for my own. I wished I'd never thought to borrow that library book for him. I wouldn't have thought of it if I hadn't hurt the mockingbird. But I'd have never known to take the bird to Lucas if I hadn't met him in the first place. That was the problem, really. If I'd never met him from the beginning, I wouldn't be having this trouble. Maybe that's why white folks wanted to stay separate from colored folks—to avoid all this mess.

Maybe I could start by pretending I hadn't ever met Lucas. I could pretend it hard enough to make it true, and then I'd be able to start fresh not having to worry about what he might do. That was it! I put my chicken sandwich down and got to thinking—thinking how relieved I was to have finally figured it out. I simply wouldn't know him anymore. Then I wouldn't have to worry about someone seeing us and thinking we were friends. I wouldn't have to hear him bet he could do something better than me. I wouldn't see the grin that lit up his whole face or watch his hands gently healing an animal or listen to his voice while he read a book.

I would never have to skip through the woods between the river and the fence and wonder if he'd be waiting. I'd never float down the river on a homemade raft or chuck sticks for Moses or gather food for hurt animals. I'd never again have to do any of that.

"Josephine? *Josephine!*"

I shook my head and looked up. The girls were staring at me curiously. I wondered how long they'd been calling my name.

"What?"

Bobby Sue huffed. "I said we're going to play beauty parlor after supper, and did you want to be a beautician first or a customer? Honestly, Jo."

"Sorry." I paused. A little sigh escaped from deep inside of me. "I was . . . I was thinking about something else." I looked at the girls. "I have an idea," I said. "Why don't we walk down to the river tonight? We could build boats out of twigs and race them on the current."

Bobby Sue wrinkled her forehead. "Why would we want to do that?"

I shrugged. "It might be fun. . . ."

Bobby Sue laughed. "Oh, Josephine. Don't be silly."

The other girls laughed, too, then went back to talking about the party.

❧

After school we were all to go home, gather our things, then meet at Rexall's Drugstore, where Mr. Snyder would collect us. As soon as the bell rang, I bounded out of my seat and raced for home. Mama was working overtime on a dress order at Treva Lane's, so she had arranged for Abilene to meet me when I got home.

I packed my overnight bag and gathered my blankets and wished Mama were there. It wasn't so much that I thought she'd fix how I was feeling, but there was something about how Mama would kick off her shoes and laugh that put things into balance.

"I packed you a basket of treats, case you changed you mind," Abilene said. She held the basket toward me with a mischievous grin. For some reason, the way Abilene had of treating me so kind just made me feel worse.

"Do you ever wish your husband had stayed home, 'stead of going off to Georgia to help those folks vote?" I blurted. The words were out of my mouth as quick as they flashed across my brain. Daddy would have scolded me to mind my manners, but I wanted to know.

Abilene set the basket on the table and thought for a good long time. "Don't suppose I do wish that," she said finally. "I'm sad he's gone, but I can't fault him for what he done. He done what he needed to do, for the children's sake. At the end of the day a body's got to be able to look at himself in the mirror. If a man don't have that, he don't have nothin' at all."

I nodded, chewing that over in my mind. I gave Abilene a big hug, even though I wasn't one for hugging, then gathered her basket of treats and the rest of my things. I glanced at the tree and longed for a sight of the bird. But the tree stayed empty and silent.

The walk to the drugstore seemed long. As I neared Main Street a breeze wafted by, carrying the pungent scent of red earth and pine. I lifted my nose and inhaled, thinking that up in the hills, someone was harvesting logs.

Several of the girls were at the drugstore when I arrived. "Do you smell that?" I asked.

"What?" Katie Moore asked. She took a few tentative sniffs. "I don't smell anything."

"Someone is cutting trees. Can't you smell the pine?"

"It smells weird," Martha said. She wore a scarf over her head. I saw a pink hair roller peeking out from under one corner. "Look, here comes Bobby Sue!"

I turned to see her daddy's Cadillac drive down Main Street. Bobby Sue was waving out the window. Just past the car, at the corner of Main and Second Avenue, a yellow dog bounded down the sidewalk, then turned in a happy circle and sat in the grass next to the town hall.

It was Moses. I'd heard that dogs have sharper senses than people. Moses must have smelled me or something, because he looked straight toward me, gave a bark, and wagged his tail like he expected a game of fetch or a race through the woods.

Simon and Lucas followed just behind. My eyes widened when I saw them. I watched Lucas pat Moses and tell him to stay. Then he looked at his older brother, who nodded. Lucas squared his shoulders and started walking toward the library.

Lucas would have noticed the smell of fresh pine, I thought. He'd have taken a deep breath, like he was trying to drink the air, then release it in one whoosh. He'd have bet me he could haul a pine tree faster than anyone in Keonee County, and I'd have bet him I could.

"JOSEPHINE!"

Bobby Sue was glaring at me with her arms crossed. "What are you doing? Are you coming?"

I looked at Bobby Sue and the other girls, who had piled into the Snyders' car. They were waiting for me to join them. Then I looked across the street. Lucas and Simon were climbing the steps to the library.

"Oh, hang it all." I threw my hands in the air, letting my bag and blankets fall to the ground, and took off running.

chapter eighteen

I didn't quite know what I aimed to accomplish by following Lucas and Simon into that library, but I figured I'd been in it from the beginning, so I'd better see it through to the end.

Lucas turned and saw me running toward them. He grinned, then he followed Simon through the library door. I snuck in behind and tried to stay out of the way. This wasn't my fight, after all. But Lucas was my friend.

The library was nearly deserted, with only Miss Spinnaker at the front desk keeping company with the books. Our footsteps fell muffled and hushed across the braided rugs. It seemed an odd place to stage a civil disobedience. I nearly forgot the reason I was there until Miss Spinnaker peered up from her work and saw

Simon and Lucas. Her face paled. She gave a little gasp and wrapped her arms across her chest. My thumb snuck to my mouth.

"Ma'am." Simon spoke first. "My brother here would like to request a library card so he can get some books."

Miss Spinnaker fixed her gaze on Lucas. "Is that so?" she asked in a tight voice that quavered at the ends. She stepped backward until she was pressed tight against the back side of the desk.

Lucas squared his shoulders. "Yes, ma'am," he said. "Yes, ma'am, I would."

"Well." Miss Spinnaker cleared her throat. She adjusted the collar around her neck and smoothed her skirt. She looked scared. Lucas and Simon weren't scary. Well, maybe Simon was—a little.

"You—you boys will have to leave," she said.

"Yes, ma'am," Simon said. "Soon as my brother gets a library card."

"We're plumb out of library cards," Miss Spinnaker said. "Now please leave."

My eyes widened as I stared at the librarian. Miss Spinnaker had either told a straight-out lie or she'd forgotten where she kept her cards. I squeezed my throbbing thumb in the center of my fist and took a deep breath. "Miss Spinnaker? You have more cards right there, in that box." I pointed it out to her.

"Josephine!" Miss Spinnaker said my name like she was just noticing I was there. A look of relief filled her face. She motioned me toward the desk. "Come here, child. Back here, where you'll be safe."

I took a step toward her, then stopped. *Safe from what?*

Miss Spinnaker turned to Simon and Lucas. "You boys will have to leave. Josephine was here first."

"No, ma'am, I wasn't." I shook my head. "Lucas and Simon came in before I did. Besides, I don't need any help. I already got my library card."

"Oh. My." Miss Spinnaker's face went from pale to red. She stared at me, then at Lucas and Simon. Her eyebrows drew together and her forehead bunched in a furrow of wrinkles. She whirled around and raced away from the desk and into her cubbyhole of an office. The door slammed behind her.

Lucas looked at me. "What is she gonna do?"

I shrugged. "I don't know." In all my times of coming to the library, I had never seen Miss Spinnaker do that before.

"What're you doin' here?" Simon asked.

"I know about the library," I explained. "Where they keep the books and such."

"Oh, you do?" Simon looked around at the shelves of books, then back to me. His face crinkled in what could have been a smile, except I had never before seen him smile. "You don't say?" I knew then that it was okay that I was there.

Miss Spinnaker stayed locked in her office. After several minutes, Simon sat on the floor, legs crossed in front of him. "She gotta come out sometime," he said. "I might as well be comfortable till she does."

Lucas and I followed his lead and sank to the floor. We waited what seemed like hours, but the library clock showed it had only been fifteen minutes.

"How long does this sort of thing usually take?" I asked.

Lucas shrugged. His eyes were wide, but they were losing that fearful look. "Don't rightly know," Simon said. "This is my first sit-in. It took near a year for them folks in Montgomery to beat the bus system."

"A year!" Were we going to wait in this library for a solid year?

Behind us, the library door opened. I turned to look. Sheriff Overby ambled in, arms swinging, face stern.

The sheriff! I scrambled to my feet. Simon and Lucas did the same.

"Sheriff Overby!" Miss Spinnaker emerged from her office. "Thank the Lord you are here." Her lower lip quivered, causing her chins to waggle like chicken wattle. "I have never been so upset in all of my life. These colored boys have talked back to me and refuse to leave." Miss Spinnaker seemed like she might cry.

Sheriff Overby looked at Simon and Lucas. "You boys best run along home now. Don't want no trouble. Hear me?" The sheriff brushed a tiny piece of lint off his sleeve as he spoke.

Simon stood taller. He thrust out his chin. Lucas watched his brother, then mimicked him.

"Run along home," the sheriff repeated, looking down at them.

I couldn't bear it. "All they did was ask for a library card."

Miss Spinnaker inhaled sharply. "Josephine! What are you saying?" She shot me a look of pure venom. I drew back. That look pierced me with fear. All at once I knew that by stepping into that library, I had done something that I could never undo. I didn't know just then if it was a good thing I had done or a bad. But I knew that I was suddenly scared. As scared as I had ever been in my life.

"Josephine Clawson," the sheriff said. "What are you doing in the middle of this mess? Does your daddy know you're here?"

I shook my head. No one knew I was here. I had promised not to tell. "All Lucas wants is a library card," I repeated softly.

"We ain't leaving till my brother gets a card," Simon said. He stood firm and solid. I guessed it would take someone a lot bigger than Sheriff Overby to move him.

"Did you hear that?" Miss Spinnaker whirled on Sheriff Overby. Her spectacles bounced on her chest. "They are trespassing! This library is not intended for coloreds. They don't belong here and I want them to leave." Twin spots of color burned in Miss Spinnaker's cheeks.

"All I want is a library card," Lucas said. "I ain't gonna hurt nothin'."

"Sheriff!" Miss Spinnaker yelled. I wondered if she might faint. I had once seen an old lady get so worked up over a stolen apple pie recipe that she fainted dead away. Mama had to revive her with smelling salts and a cold washcloth.

"Come on, boys." The sheriff motioned them out.

"We ain't moving," Simon repeated.

"Josephine, get on out of here," the sheriff said. "I don't want you to see this."

I stood caught between the sheriff and Lucas. I took a step closer to Lucas and Simon.

"All they want is to get some books." I licked my lips. My mouth was suddenly dry.

"Arrest them!" Miss Spinnaker demanded. She leaned heavily against her desk and patted her heart. "They can't come in here like this. It isn't decent. I'm a God-fearing woman. . . ."

"Aw, they're just being foolish . . . ," the sheriff said.

"Arrest them!" Miss Spinnaker repeated. She straightened, like she had regained some of her strength. "I'm pressing charges. Trespassing, disorderly conduct, unseemly behavior, unlawful fraternizing." She gave me a look that made me feel suddenly dirty. I wanted to swallow, but I didn't have any spit in my mouth.

The sheriff sighed. "Don't you want to calm down and think about this?"

"No! Arrest them. Get them out of my library!"

I watched in mute horror as Sheriff Overby approached Simon and snapped handcuffs on his wrists. Simon didn't make a move. The sheriff prodded him in the back with his nightstick, and Simon lurched forward.

"You too," the sheriff told Lucas. He waved his nightstick at him.

"And Josephine." Miss Spinnaker stared at me with utter hatred. My eyes opened wide.

"Josephine?"

"She was part of it. She was keeping company with these boys. Arrest her, too. Maybe it will serve to teach her a much needed lesson. Preacher's daughter, indeed!"

My gut squeezed up in a tight little knot. My feet tingled. I wanted to run. I wanted to run as far away from that library as I could get. Run clear out of town, deep into the woods, all the way to the fence.

I didn't look at Miss Spinnaker. I couldn't meet her eyes. Instead I looked at Lucas. I could tell he was scared, too. His forehead pinched together, making creases between his eyes, and sweat beaded above his upper lip. He didn't look ready to run, though. Not like me. He stood straight and tall, like his brother.

Then Sheriff Overby motioned with his nightstick. I allowed myself to be directed out the door.

I was going to jail.

chapter nineteen

It was only a few steps from the library to the city jail just next door, but it seemed like we walked for miles. A few curious eyes peeked out of passing cars and nearby stores to see what was happening. I stared at the ground. I was a criminal. I had shamed the Lord Almighty. Daddy was going to kill me.

I thought about making a run for it. I wasn't handcuffed, only Simon. I could have turned and bolted for the woods. But Sheriff Overby had his nightstick and his gun. I wondered if he'd shoot me if I tried to escape.

The thought made my blood run cold.

Lucas stumbled on the step leading to the jailhouse. He pitched forward and cracked his forehead on the railing. I gasped. Lucas didn't make a sound.

"Are you okay?" the sheriff asked. He helped Lucas

steady himself, then peered at the scrape on Lucas's forehead. "Let's get inside and clean that up."

Sheriff Overby directed us into the jail. It was a large, square room made of concrete cinder blocks. The walls were painted a putrid shade of green. It made me feel sick to my stomach. Two cells with iron bars lined one wall. Sheriff Overby steered Simon into one cell and me into the other.

"Peppermint?" he offered as he settled me into the cell. He reached one hand into his pocket.

I shook my head.

The sheriff got a wet washcloth and some gauze to bandage Lucas's forehead. Then Lucas went into the cell with Simon. The sheriff offered them each a peppermint, too. They declined.

Sheriff Overby stared at us for a few minutes, shook his head, then walked to the desk. "I don't want trouble," he said. "This here's a peaceful town. Folks get along just fine. Not like that mess in Little Rock." The sheriff looked at Simon and Lucas, then began straightening the papers on his desk. "No cause for you boys to start acting up."

Simon and Lucas didn't say anything to that. Sheriff Overby directed his attention to me. "How did you get mixed up in this, Josephine?"

I shrugged. It was a long story.

"I'm going to call your father."

I sank onto the cot in the corner of the cell and closed my eyes. *Daddy. What would he do when he found out I was in jail? What would Mama do?* I choked back a sob. I couldn't let Lucas or Simon hear me cry.

The sheriff picked up the phone. I heard him ask the operator to ring Daddy. I groaned. Now the whole town would know. I listened in despair as the sheriff tried to tell Daddy what had happened.

"Have your daughter," he said. "Here at the jail. . . . No, no, nothing like that. Disturbance at the library. . . . Lucas and Simon Jeffer—" The sheriff's voice was growing increasingly flustered. "They were at the lib . . . right, I have them here. . . . Yes, Josephine, too."

The sheriff pulled back and looked at the phone with a bewildered look on his face. Then he hung it up and began polishing his desktop.

No one said anything. The minutes ticked by slowly on the clock above his desk. Twenty minutes passed in this way, long enough for me to think about what I had done. A part of me wished I had gone to Bobby Sue's party. I'd be there now, playing beauty parlor and dress up. Instead I was locked up. Maybe I'd be here forever. I snuck a look at Lucas. He was leaning against the wall in the other cell. He caught my eye.

"Civil disobedience," he mouthed.

I forced my lips up at the corners, but I just couldn't smile.

The door clanged open. Daddy stormed inside. I rose to my feet. "Josephine!" Daddy hollered. He looked at the sheriff, then charged toward the desk. "What is the meaning of this?" he demanded. "Why is my daughter locked in that cell?"

Sheriff Overby stood. "Like I tried to explain on the phone," he said. "She was in the library with these Negro boys." He motioned toward Lucas and Simon. Daddy gave them a quick glance. "It seems they tried to get a library card."

"A library card?" Daddy's voice was incredulous.

"Well, yes. You see—"

"Is it suddenly illegal to go to the library?" Daddy exploded. His face was red and puffing.

"Is for coloreds." The sheriff stuck out his chin, but then wilted under Daddy's glare. "They were trespassing. And disturbin' the, uh, peace." The sheriff stuttered. He seemed to shrink under Daddy's thundering.

"They are children!" Daddy bellowed.

"Well, well, yes, sir, of course . . ."

"Josephine is eleven years old. Not a one of them is above seventeen!" He gave a quick look to Simon as if to confirm that fact. Then he turned back to the sheriff.

"Do you mean to tell me these children have been arrested?"

I shuddered.

"Well, have they?" Daddy bellowed again. I raised my head to look.

"Well, not exactly. That is, Miss Spinnaker said she wanted to press charges. But she was upset. I was just holding them until she calmed down a bit."

Daddy let out a long sigh. He sank into a chair opposite the sheriff's desk.

"That's my little girl," he said.

The sheriff nodded.

"And those boys, they're good boys. Got a good mama."

The sheriff nodded again. "Never expected nothing like this out of them. Although with what their father done . . ."

"It was a library card," Daddy said.

"Library is white only," the sheriff replied. "Ain't no Supreme Court told us to integrate the library." He cocked his head. "Did they?"

Daddy shook his head. Then he rubbed his face and felt his scar.

"Release them to me," Daddy said. "I'll take them."

"Your daughter, certainly, sir, but . . ."

"Release them all to me. The boys, too. I'll see that they get home. Release them, now."

Daddy didn't have to say "or else." He was boiling mad. The sheriff fumbled with his keys.

"You're responsible for them," the sheriff mumbled to Daddy.

The clank of the lock opening on my cell sent a wave of joy clear through me. The sheriff unlocked the other cell, but Simon refused to move.

"I've got to stand firm," he said to Daddy. "I'm gonna stay in jail and make my point."

"Your point has been made, son. And you can make it again tomorrow and the next day and for all eternity if you like. But you might as well make your point as a free man."

Simon thought that over for a moment, then nodded. He followed Daddy.

On the way out Daddy turned back to the sheriff. "See to it that no one lays a hand on these boys tonight or tomorrow night or ever. I want them protected."

I looked at Simon and Lucas. Protected?

"Oh, yes, sir," he said. "I'll make sure of that. Don't want no trouble. This here's a peaceful town."

Daddy marched out of the jailhouse, down the steps, and across Main Street. Simon, Lucas, and I hustled after him like ducks in a row. Lucas whistled and Moses raced to his side. I could hear Daddy muttering, but I couldn't understand what he was saying. Finally, when we reached Plantation Drive, he slowed and allowed us to catch up. Daddy studied each one of us in turn. Simon and Lucas met his gaze, but my eyes shifted away.

"What happened to your head?" Daddy asked Lucas.

"Fell, sir," he said. "Bumped it."

"Hurt?"

"No, sir."

"And all you wanted was a library card?" Daddy asked.

"Yes, sir."

"You didn't go in there yelling or screaming or pulling books down?"

"Daddy!" I said. "He was polite as could be. He even said please."

Daddy ignored me and looked back at Lucas.

"Can you read?"

I flinched with embarrassment. Lucas narrowed his eyes and nodded. "Yes, sir."

"Y'all don't have your own library, then?"

"No, sir," Lucas said. "We don't got much of any-thin'."

"I want my brother to have a chance to get learnin'," Simon said. "He is powerful smart."

Daddy shook his head and mumbled something that sounded a bit like swearing.

We walked in silence for a while. "Sir?" Lucas asked. "Do you s'pose I'll ever get one? A library card, that is?"

Daddy stopped walking and gave him a serious look. "That I don't know, son," he said to Simon. "It won't be easy. Are you sure you really want it?"

Simon's eyes flashed and his shoulders stiffened. "Yes, sir."

"Yes, sir," Lucas repeated.

"Well, then, one of these days you most certainly will get one."

Lucas's face shined like it was Christmas and his birthday all rolled into one.

We reached the fork in the road. "Come with us to our house, please," Daddy asked Simon and Lucas. "I want you to walk your mother home."

They nodded. We continued down the street until we reached the back door of the parsonage. Mama hustled outside, followed by Miz Abilene. Abilene's eyes lit up when she saw her boys. She raced to them and wrapped them in a hug. Her face looked drawn and worried.

"Take care of your mama," Daddy told Simon.

"Yes, sir."

Mama pulled me to her and kissed the top of my head. "You're almost too tall for me to do that," she murmured.

I stood at the back door between Mama and Daddy. We watched as Miz Abilene and her two sons and Moses set off down Plantation Drive toward the colored quarters. Lucas waved his hands wildly as they walked. I guessed he was telling Miz Abilene about going to jail.

Mama kicked off her shoes. Daddy turned to her. He looked her up and down, then turned to look at me. He opened his mouth to speak, then closed it again. I wondered if I was about to get hollered at or spanked, but Daddy just rubbed his chin.

"A library card," he said finally.

Mama didn't say a word, just squeezed my shoulder as we walked inside.

chapter twenty

I stayed in my room and read most of Saturday. It wasn't until after lunch that I realized the book I was reading was from the library. I didn't know how I felt about that.

The phone rang all day, but Mama or Daddy always answered and spoke in quiet tones so I couldn't hear what was being said. One time I overheard Daddy talking to Mama. "It will tear this town in two," Daddy said.

"You know she was right."

"No one cares about what's right."

"All the more reason why we should."

Daddy didn't answer, the house got quiet, and I went back to watching the tree and wishing the mockingbird would come home. I missed Lucas and hoped he was okay. I decided that I'd check out library books for him every week, if I had to.

Daddy woke early on Sunday morning, which wasn't so unusual. What was unusual was how loudly he was stomping about. He was sure to wake Mama. I climbed out of bed and tiptoed to the kitchen. Daddy was sitting at the table and staring at his Bible. Every now and then he'd shake his head and grumble, like he and that Bible were having some sort of argument.

Daddy stood and slammed the Bible closed. "Of all things!" he said. He stomped to his bedroom and I followed along behind. Daddy hadn't yet noticed me.

"Come on, Maye, wake up," Daddy said. "We need to fetch someone before service starts this morning."

Mama rose out of bed, a smile on her face. Then Daddy turned to me. "You," he said. "You get your clothes on, and quickly. You're a part of this, too."

I hurried to comply, though I didn't know whom we needed to get or why. It wasn't until I was settled in the backseat of Daddy's Chevy that Mama let it be known that we were going to pick up Lenore Cooper.

Lenore Cooper lived two miles past the old sawmill on a hard-packed road of red clay. I had figured she would live in a shack, but her house was a one-story clapboard with a front porch and a fresh coat of white-wash. Zinnias bloomed beside the front step. She didn't have a driveway to speak of, so we pulled into what must have been her front yard.

A face appeared in the window when we arrived, then Miss Lenore burst out the front door. I thought I would die of embarrassment when she ran to the car and gave Mama a hug. Going to jail was bad enough. Now everyone would see me and Lenore Cooper riding in the very same car. Sometimes Mama went too far with her charity cases.

Miss Lenore didn't change clothes when she learned we were going to church. She wore a simple cotton dress with nothing fancy to it at all, but she put a bright red ribbon in her daughter's dark curls. Then we piled into the Chevy and drove back to town, with nobody saying much of anything along the way. I was busy thinking how I might explain things to Bobby Sue. First jail, then Lenore Cooper. It wasn't going to be easy.

I felt something brush against my leg. I looked down and saw Lenore Cooper's little girl patting me with a plump hand. She glanced shyly at me and gave a little smile. I smiled back. I couldn't help it. Her fat cheeks dimpled.

It wasn't fair, I thought suddenly. Her being shamed for something she had no part of. And she was such a happy little girl. I couldn't help but like her. I reached into my pocket and took out a shiny nickel, one I'd been saving for the offering. I held it toward her. She giggled, then pointed toward the nickel with a chubby finger.

"You can have it," I said.

The little girl looked quickly toward her mother. "Mine?" she asked.

Her mother shook her head. "Oh, no. That's too much. . . ."

"Really," I said. "She can have it."

"Mine." The little girl took the nickel and turned it over and over in her tiny hands. I watched her and for a moment forgot about my embarrassment; then we pulled into the church parking lot and it returned in a panic. I scrunched down in my seat. What would people be saying about me?

"I don't feel good," I managed to whisper to Mama. "I need to go home." I wasn't lying. I felt like I was going to be sick.

"You get out of this car and march into that church," Mama said.

"But Mama, I'm sick!"

"What you are is scared."

"They're all going to look at me," I said.

"Then let them look."

"But Mama . . ."

Mama wrapped me in a quick, fierce hug. "I'm

proud of you, baby girl," she whispered. "No matter what anyone says. Now you stay brave."

There was no arguing. I wrapped my arms around my stomach and tried to keep myself from throwing up. Then we all walked toward the church, Daddy, Mama, Lenore Cooper, her little girl, and me. I stared at the ground, carefully watching my feet and trying not to listen to the whispers and the snickers that hummed around us.

Bobby Sue and her friends stood in a cluster at the bottom of the front steps. I froze when I saw them. Mama nudged me forward.

"Look. It's 'Jailhouse Rock,'" Martha Pierson whispered, loud enough for me to hear. Katie Moore laughed and started humming the Elvis song.

I clenched my jaw and pretended I hadn't heard.

"Jo." It was Bobby Sue. I stopped and looked at her. She stared at me with a puzzled frown on her face.

"Did you memorize the verse for class?" she asked.

I had to think for a minute. I wasn't expecting the question. "Yes," I said. It was a verse from Acts, when God tells the apostle Peter to go to the gentiles. We were studying Peter in class. He was my favorite disciple. And, as I suddenly remembered, he also had been thrown in jail. "I did."

"Me too," she said. "I memorized it, too." Then she

turned back to her friends. Mama put her hand on my shoulder, and we walked up the steps to the church.

Daddy opened the front doors and ushered us inside. I followed Mama. We made our way to the front for the opening announcements. I heard the rest of the congregation file in behind us. Daddy walked toward us, then took his place at the chair behind the pulpit. His only job during opening announcements was to welcome new visitors. Today was the first time he'd had any visitors to welcome.

The deacon chairman's wife and two women from the Ladies' Aid walked up the aisle. They stopped and glared at us before turning toward their seats. "I have never been so disgusted in my life," the deacon chairman's wife huffed.

"The apple doesn't fall far from the tree," another woman said.

I cringed and glanced at Mama. Her eyes looked pained.

I reached over and slipped my hand into Mama's. "I'm sorry," I whispered.

She squeezed my hand. "You're not the one who needs to be sorry."

Lenore Cooper touched Mama's arm, then leaned over and whispered something in her ear. Mama grinned. The look of sadness left her eyes. Mama whispered something back.

I watched Mama and Lenore Cooper whispering back and forth while Brother Barnaby Baxter droned on and on with announcements. Lenore Cooper sure didn't act like one of Mama's charity cases, I thought. She acted like . . .

The thought stopped me cold. Lenore Cooper and Mama were acting like *friends*.

Brother Baxter started to pray. I didn't bow my head, didn't even close my eyes. I stared at Mama and Miss Lenore and wondered if it could be true. Could they be friends? But why? Why would Mama be friends with her? She had to know that people would gossip and stare.

I listened in a haze to the rest of the prayer and then to Daddy when he stood to introduce Lenore Cooper. Everybody already knew who she was, but it was Daddy's job to welcome her anyway.

No one clapped after the introductions or made a move to greet Miss Lenore. In fact, the congregation sat frozen, staring straight ahead and not making a sound, until Brother Baxter reminded everyone it was time for Sunday school.

I made my way downstairs to my class. The stares

and whispers of the other kids were hurtful. I took a seat in the back row. No one, not even Miss Hasty, motioned me toward the front. Bobby Sue looked my way, once, after she recited the memory verse, and gave me what could have been a smile. I blinked and couldn't think fast enough to smile back. Mostly I was wondering about Mama and Lenore Cooper. Mama could be friends with anyone she wanted, I thought. Why would she choose Lenore Cooper?

Daddy preached on Loving Our Neighbor during the sermon time. His words were as powerful as ever. They made me think of Miz Abilene's gentle hands as they brewed a yarrow tea, and of the furrow in Lucas's forehead when he tended to the mockingbird, and of the jasmine smell of Mama when she came home from work. Mostly they made me think of the friends I had made in Jericho, and they made me start to understand Mama a little bit more.

chapter twenty-one

I left for the river as soon as Sunday dinner had finished. I had never been on a Sunday. It didn't seem right before, but now it felt like the perfect place to be.

The wind sighed in the trees. It smelled of fall—of harvesttime and brilliant leaves and crisp, cool nights. I perched on the fallen log and prepared to wait. The river burbled beneath me.

I don't know how long I sat there on that log, but I finally saw him. Lucas trod through the woods wearing black pants and a white shirt. I guessed he had just come from church. Moses ambled beside him.

Lucas raised a hand in greeting, then sat beside me on the log. Neither one of us spoke for a few moments. We sat in uneasy silence and watched the river flow past.

I had a million questions. A million things I wanted to say. "Did you get in trouble?" I asked. "About the library?"

Lucas shook his head. "No. But folks are talkin' 'bout it somethin' fierce."

I nodded. I knew what that was like.

"Did you? Get in trouble?" Lucas asked.

"No. But . . ." There were so many *buts*. Things would never be the same. Not with me, not with my family, not with Jericho. And probably not with Lucas. "No, I didn't get in trouble."

"Someone threw rocks at our house," Lucas said. "But they didn't break nothin'."

"Rocks? Who did?"

Lucas shrugged. "Dunno. It was dark."

I shivered. "You going back? To the library?"

"Me and Simon were talkin'. We gotta go back. Got to figure out how to do it. Simon says he wishes some of those reporters down in Little Rock would come and see."

"Why?"

"Simon says it'd make a difference if we were in pictures."

I thought about that for a minute. "I'll check out books for you, as long as you like."

Lucas shrugged. "I'd rather get them myself."

"I know." I kicked at the leaf-strewn ground, then turned to Lucas. "Bet I can run to the fence faster than you."

"Can not!" Lucas declared.

"Race you, then." I grinned and leapt off the rock. Lucas scrambled next to me. I took a ready stance.

"On your mark, get set, GO!"

I tore through the woods, kicking up leaves and red mud. My skirt swirled around my legs. I could hear Lucas behind me, then Moses, barking. The wind whipped my hair. I was running faster than I had ever run. I raced through brush and dodged tree roots.

"Jo!" Lucas yelled. I glanced back and put on an extra burst of speed, not willing to give an inch. My skirt tangled around my legs. I looked down, trying to wrest it free with one hand. I wasn't going to let it stop me. *I was going to win!*

"JO!"

I looked up and the fence was suddenly upon me, rushing full tilt. I tried to slow, but my skirt tripped up my legs. I stuck out my hands, trying to brace myself against the barbed wire. At the moment of impact I closed my eyes.

I felt a sting as wire pierced skin, then a bone-jolting thud as my body connected with the fence. The world turned upside down. I found myself tumbling forward through grass and mud and wood. I landed on my back with an *oomph*.

When I opened my eyes, I saw Lucas standing in the middle of broken boards, looking down at me.

I took several gasping breaths. It felt like all the air had been knocked clean out of my lungs. "What happened?" I asked. I was staring into the clear blue of the sky and wondering if I should move. I inventoried my body, carefully checking if anything was broken. Everything felt bruised.

"You okay?" Lucas inched over to me. He held out his hand. I let him pull me to a sitting position. I blinked, clearing my vision.

"What happened?" I asked again.

"You hurled yourself at that fence like you'd gone plumb crazy," Lucas said. "It's a wonder you're still alive."

"Did I win?"

Lucas shook his head. "You won, all right. Near killed yourself doing it. And look what you've done. Broke the fence clean apart."

I looked around me. He was right. A section of the fence had cracked and toppled to the ground. Lucas and I sat in a pile of splintered wood and snarls of barbed wire. Just beyond, the fence stretched unbroken to the horizon. But around me and Lucas, all that remained was rubble.

I remembered what Daddy had said, that it'd take blood and tears to bring the fence down.

"You need a bandage for your arm," Lucas said. He pointed to a long gash that was oozing blood. I studied the cut, then noticed a rip in the hem of my blouse. It was stained red.

"It's okay."

"Yarrow'll keep it from getting infected," Lucas said. "Y'all got some at home? Mama does, I know. You should get on home and get that cleaned up." He fussed over my arm. His face wore that look of concern and care I had come to know.

"I will. In a minute." My cuts and bruises throbbed. I knew I'd have to go home and explain to Mama and Daddy what had happened, why I was so banged up. But something in me didn't want to leave the woods and the river and that broken-down fence. Not just yet.

I wanted to remember everything the way it was at just that moment. The wind ruffling through the trees, the river gurgling off in the distance, the feel of Lucas sitting beside me in a heap of wood and rubble. And off in the trees, a bird singing *teel-a-wheet, teel-a-wheet* with all its might.

I didn't know how much longer we'd stay in Jericho. Daddy had crossed an invisible line by introducing Lenore Cooper in church that morning, and me and Mama with him. No one nodded or said "amen!" when he preached on loving our neighbors. All he got were cold, hard stares. I wondered if the deacons would vote him out. That had never happened to Daddy before. He had always gotten a call from God to go elsewhere first. But this time was different.

"Look." Lucas touched me on the arm and pointed. A bird perched on a splintered fence post only a few feet away. "It's our mockingbird."

A thrill went through me at the sight of that bird. I realized how much I had missed him. Lucas and I sat silent and still. The mockingbird ruffled his tail and cocked his head, peering at us with quick, bright eyes. Then he opened his mouth to sing.

It was a song I had never heard before, trilling and pure with a rhythm that, strangely enough, made me want to dance.

"That's no birdsong I ever knew," Lucas whispered.

I shook my head. It wasn't. It was a song of the mockingbird's very own.

The bird sang, and it seemed the world held its breath just to listen. Then the bird gave a hop and a twitch and flew into the air.

"You healed him," I said to Lucas.

Lucas stood and stared after the bird. Then he grabbed my hand and pulled me to my feet. We stepped over broken fence rails and walked in silence through the woods, still listening for the song of the mockingbird.

I thought, as we walked, that life must be like the mockingbird's song—mostly just mimicking the notes and rhythms of other folks and not thinking twice about it—until the day you make up your very own song and decide that's the one you have to sing. At least, that's how it felt to me, that summer in Jericho.

Author's Note

Although the events and characters in *Jericho Walls* are fictional, it is loosely based on stories my mother told me about what it was like growing up the daughter of a preacher in the South in the 1950s. Like Jo, she was expected to be good and proper and to know her memory verses. Also like Jo, her family moved often and she had to give up many friends and activities along the way. To fill the times of loneliness, my mother read books and explored the woods, lakes, and scrublands of the South. She also occasionally got herself into trouble.

It is true that in much of the South during the 1950s, African Americans faced extreme discrimination. They were not allowed to attend the same schools as white children or to use the same libraries, drinking fountains, restaurants, or rest rooms. Many communities passed laws prohibiting the "fraternizing" of the races, meaning that it would have been illegal for Jo and Lucas to be friends. White children often attended large, well-equipped modern schools, while the schools of African-American children often didn't have enough money for books or teachers. It was very difficult for many African-American men to find jobs that would support their families.

Several of the events in this book are based on history. In 1956, Rosa Parks refused to give up her seat to a white man and sparked the Montgomery bus boycott. This protest gained national attention and landed Dr. Martin Luther King, Jr., on the cover of *Time* magazine for his role in the civil rights movement. In September 1957, nine African-American children faced threats, harassment, and the Arkansas National Guard when they bravely began the integration of Central High School in Little Rock, Arkansas.

While there were a few white preachers in the South who believed the church was called to fight discrimination, they were unfortunately the exception. Like Daddy in this book, many were born into a culture where segregation was the accepted way of life. It was difficult and scary to challenge that thinking.

But there were also people like Mama in this book. People who had witnessed bigotry and intolerance and knew that it was wrong. One of those people was my grandmother, who had seen the abuse leveled against her grandmother, a Native American. My grandmother knew that friendship wasn't based on the color of a person's skin, but on the character of a person's heart. There are also millions like Lucas, Simon, Abilene, and her husband who had the courage to say, "This is wrong. Let's change this." Those who spoke out against racism and discrimination rarely made it into the history books, but they made a difference all the same.

Many people lost their lives in the civil rights movement. Others lost their homes, their jobs, and their churches. They made sacrifices because they strongly believed in freedom and equality. Today, those people are heroes. At the time, they were ordinary men, women, and children who had the courage to take a stand against injustice.

DATE DUE
